MW00987124

RODEO *Heat*

DESIREE HOLT

ELLORA'S CAVE
ROMANTICA PUBLISHING

An Ellora's Cave Romantica Publication

www.ellorascave.com

Rodeo Heat

ISBN 9781419961298
ALL RIGHTS RESERVED.
Rodeo Heat Copyright © 2010 Desiree Holt
Edited by Helen Woodall.
Cover art by Syneca.

Electronic book publication September 2009
Trade paperback publication 2010

RODEO HEAT

 හ

Dedication

෨

This book is dedicated to our very wonderful and elegant Martha Punches, a personal role model for us all, who keeps us straight, handles us with care and brings us sunshine even in the rain. Bless you, Martha. You light all our candles.

Trademarks Acknowledgement

෨

The author acknowledges the trademarked status and trademark owners of the following wordmarks mentioned in this work of fiction:

Keurig: Green Mountain Coffee, Inc.

Lone Star beer: Olympia Brewing Company

Play-Doh: Hasbro Inc. Corporation

Stetson: John B. Stetson Company

Styrofoam: The Dow Chemical Company

The Riverwalk: El Paseo Del Rio, Inc.

UPS: United Parcel Service of America, Inc.

Chapter One

ဆ

They were in the huge coliseum building where the rodeo vendors were set up, right next to the huge rodeo arena. The air was filled with a raucous blend of shouts and laughter, the air heavy with the mingled scents of horses, cattle, manure and hay that drifted in through the huge open doors. Grace Delaney figured there were at least two thousand people jammed into a space where half that number could barely fit comfortably.

She stood in front of the makeshift mirror at the vendor's booth tilting the cowgirl hat she was trying on this way and that. Her western-style shirt and prewashed jeans looked like a costume she'd borrowed from someone else and her new boots were pinching her toes. Torn between a suddenly emerging need for adventure and a lifetime of playing it safe, she'd let her closest friend, Melanie Keyes, drag her to a Western store and outfit her, then agreed to come to the rodeo with her. Now the habits of more than twenty years were rearing their heads and misgivings were crowding in on her like a flock of geese.

"I wish I knew how in the hell I let you talk me into this," she muttered.

"Because you need to have some spice in your life." Melanie Aldrich lifted a hot pink hat from the display stand and set it firmly on her tousled blonde curls, then turned to Grace. "What do you think?"

"I think I should have stayed home," Grace told her, removing the hat from her own head. "I must be crazy. This isn't me. Hanging out at rodeos and displaying myself for the cowboys like a piece of meat. You know that, Mel."

Melanie grabbed her by the shoulders and gave her a stern look.

"Listen, Grace. We've been friends since fifth grade and you've never taken a chance in your life. I watched you dive into a 'safe' marriage, one that wouldn't unlock the part of yourself I know you hide inside."

"But I loved Joe," she began.

"I know, I know. But it was a safe love, whether you want to admit it or not. I watched you pull yourself together when Joe died and build a life for yourself and your kids. I watched you choose a 'safe'—make that dull—career in accounting so you could put numbers in squares just like you've done with every day of your life. And when, after eighteen years, you finally decided to date again, you picked men twenty years older than you. 'Safe' again. I'll bet they can't even get it up without a big supply of those little blue pills. Come on. 'Fess up. I'm right, aren't I?"

Grace blew out a breath. Sometimes she didn't know whether to hug Melanie or kill her. The problem was, in this instance she was completely right and Grace hated that. So what if she was forty-four and boring. It was better than being divorced three times and running around with one gorgeous but unreliable man after another like Melanie did. Wasn't it? Well, wasn't it?

But even she had been smart enough to know her life needed something besides spreadsheets and men with clammy hands. Joe had died before they'd ever had a chance to fully explore their sexual relationship and for more than twenty years she'd been completely celibate. One day when she was passing an adult entertainment store, her car turned in as if it had a life of its own and she'd left with a collection of erotic books and movies that would have made a hooker blush.

Driven by her suddenly awakened curiosity, she huddled in her bedroom each night, reading until her eyes blurred and watching the movies until her eyes popped out and she found herself blushing. Like an addict seeking more drugs, she went back to the store again and again, her secret collection growing as her brain struggled to absorb the things people did with and to each other in their sexual encounters.

The things the authors described hadn't even been on her radar screen. She'd never be brave enough to try any of those things in real life but at least she was expanding her horizons. If she couldn't do it, she could read about it. But as she lost herself in page after page and in scene after scene she found herself aroused, turned on, squeezing her legs to still the throbbing in her cunt, so she invested in a couple of toys that she used to relieve the tension when she needed to.

"Glad to see you spicing up your life," the clerk told her the last time she rang up her purchases.

Grace lowered her eyes and nearly ran from the store. What was it with everyone wanting to "spice" things up for her? Was she flashing a sign that said "boring"?

Now, however, she had quite a collection of books and movies, each one introducing her to new and different sexual pleasures. She kept the books and DVDs hidden in her closet, dragging them out at night with the bedroom door locked. Not that there was anyone left in the house to even pay attention. She'd been reading her latest, appropriately titled *Ride Me, Cowboy*, with a naked cowboy on the cover, when Melanie had called to talk her into this little excursion and she hadn't been able to say no.

So here she was, decked out in her new threads, being pushed for the first time in her life into something daring and wondering what kind of fool she'd make of herself. Or if she even had the courage to try. Her mind and body were busy doing battle with each other. But...she guessed she had to start somewhere to step outside the lines, even if it was only buying a new outfit.

"That hat is so you," Melanie gushed. "I'm buying it for you. Put it back on your head."

"But—"

"But nothing. I'm still spending Langford Keyes' more than generous divorce settlement. Take it while I've got it, honey."

"I thought we were here to see the rodeo." Grace hurried to keep up with her friend who was sashaying—that was the only word for it—her way through the crowds of people. "So far all we've done is shop."

"We will, sweetie. We will. But shopping's half the fun. I want to stop at a little booth I hit every year. This woman sells the most fantastic jewelry, some of it very old. And she always has a story to tell about each piece."

Grace shook her head but followed Melanie halfway around the barn until her friend found the vendor's booth she was looking for. She and the woman greeted each other like long-lost friends, hugging and gushing. Grace sighed and distracted herself by looking at the jewelry displayed on the table.

"Oh miss." The woman reached out and touched her arm. "Look. This is perfect for you. I feel a connection."

She held out her other hand, palm open. An exquisite pin in the shape of a boot lay nestled there. A tiny silver rowel clung to the heel, which was scored to show the lines so commonly seen. The brilliance of newness had faded with age and now it glowed with a smooth patina that sparkled and warmed. As if pulled by a string, Grace reached out for it and at once felt a warmth on her skin that raced through her body.

What the hell?

"It is for you," the woman told her. "You must have it. I tell you, I feel the connection for you. This pin has a long history of bringing lovers together."

"Oh no," Grace protested. "I'm not—"

"That's true," the woman said with a knowing look. "But there is a hidden longing, a sense of desire. This pin will unlock those doors you hide behind."

Grace wanted to run away. How dare this woman talk to her like in such a personal manner?

But the woman gripped her hand. "I will charge you very little but if you pass it up, you will miss meeting the most extraordinary man ever."

Grace stared at the pin, mesmerized by the feel of it, at the same time thinking, *It will take more than a pin to do something about my pitiful sex life.*

Not that the choice wasn't hers. As it had been for the past twenty years. But her new taste in reading had made her do some uncomfortable thinking. Somewhere she'd lost her sexuality and looking for it was a task that would move her out of her comfort zone, a terrifying thought.

"Oh buy it, Grace," Melanie enthused, interrupting her thoughts. "No. Wait. I want to buy it for you. You're so practical you'll walk away from it."

"Sensible," Grace corrected. "And I'm not looking for an 'extraordinary' man."

I don't even know what "extraordinary" is anymore.

"And that's the problem," Melanie said. "It's well past time you found one." "There. Now we just need to follow its lead." She fastened the pin on Grace's shirt, patting it with her hand.

The moment the pin touched her again the same blaze of heat shot through her, stirring her pulses and making her weak-kneed. Grace had never believed in omens or good luck charms or anything so fanciful but somehow she couldn't make herself remove the pin.

"Okay, let's go." Melanie tucked her purchase in her purse and took Grace by the arm. "Now we hit the big barn where the guys eat. I promised a special honey that I'd pop by and give him a kiss."

Grace tried to huff and walk at the same time. "I swear to god, Melanie. Is this another one of your boy toy trophies?

And what do I do while you and he make eyes at each other? Or whatever else you plan to do."

Melanie laughed as she headed for an exit. "He's an old acquaintance, honey, whom I've enjoyed a lot of good times with. And while I'm reminiscing with him, you'll be scoping the room for your own trophy. And it's surely about time. Just remember the pin."

How did I ever let Melanie talk me into this?

They were in a hallway leading to the next building, Melanie bouncing along in front of her, chattering a mile a minute, when Grace spotted a rodeo poster tacked on the wall and stopped dead. A dark-haired, dark-eyed cowboy in the classic pose on a bucking horse, arm extended in the air for balance, stared down at her. If he wasn't the naked man on the cover of the book she'd been reading just last night, he was so close to it they could be twins.

The pin on her blouse seemed to blossom with heat and in an instant she was back in the pages of the story, in the scene she'd read over and over again, wishing the heroine was her.

* * * * *

The ranch hands had been out there a long time, Dalton riding right beside his men as they moved the cattle to the winter pasture. Running a herd was hard work but Carrie had grown up on a ranch so she was used to it. Sometimes, when Dalton was checking the calves or taking a turn riding fence she rode along with him.

But today was their second anniversary and she'd stayed behind to prepare a special surprise for him. The closing of the back door signaled his return and in a moment she heard the thunk of his boots on the hardwood floor.

"Sweetheart? You upstairs?"

Then the sound of his footsteps on the stairs.

She was waiting for him at the door to their bedroom, wearing nothing but a big smile. Dalton's eyes widened as he spotted her and a huge, wicked grin split his face.

"This was definitely worth waiting for, sugar." He lowered his head to lick her nipples and ran the fingers of one hand through her almost bare slit. "Mmm," he moaned as he licked his fingers clean. "Delicious as always but the first thing I have to do is wash away all the cow stink. I don't know how I'm going to control myself long enough to do that."

She reached out a hand to him. "Lucky for you I've got that covered."

She led him into the bedroom where she quickly stripped away his jacket and placed his hat on the dresser. As he toed off his boots she unbuttoned his work shirt, taking her time to run her fingers through the fine pelt of dark hair on his chest and graze her fingernails over his nipples. He tried to reach for her hands but she batted him away.

"Uh-uh. This is my show." She stood on tiptoe to nip at his chin. "Happy anniversary, Dalton."

When she had the shirt completely unbuttoned she yanked it from his jeans and tossed it to the side with his jacket. As she began to work on his belt buckle, she bent her head and took first one then the other of his nipples into her mouth, nibbling at them, then lapping at them with her tongue.

His hands gripped her shoulders. "You're killing me, sugar. Please let me just get rid of these clothes and jump in the shower. I can't stand not to touch all your sweet naked flesh."

"Be patient," she teased, pulling the belt free of its loops. "There'll be plenty of time for touching. And other things."

The sound of his zipper being lowered was loud in the room. Kneeling down, she licked a line across the top of his waistband, then pushed the denim fabric down his hips, taking his boxers with them. His thick erection sprang proud and free from its sheltering nest of curls, the broad head already deepening to a dark purple. A teasing smile curving her lips, she wrapped her small fingers around his cock, bent her head and swiped her tongue across the velvet surface, catching the drop of fluid that sat atop the slit. For good measure she probed the slit with the tip of her tongue, then sucked the head into her mouth.

"Jesus!" He pulled her head away from him. "In a minute I'll forget myself and fuck you right here on the floor."

She looked up and let his cock slip from the tight clasp of her lips. "Now that would spoil all the fun, cowboy."

Standing, she took his hand and led him into the huge bathroom, part of the new master suite they'd recently added on. Fat candles shimmered on every surface, filling the air with traces of vanilla and fragrant steam rose from the large hot tub they'd had built in.

"Every cowboy should have something fancy in his life," she told him. "I thought this would be nice for our anniversary."

"You're all the fancy I need," he replied. "No shower first?"

"Oh, yeah." She winked at him. "You bet."

She turned the handle in the big shower and jets misted water at them from a dozen different directions. Urging him inside, she splashed water on him until his skin was completely wet, then grabbed the shower gel and squeezed a generous amount into the palm of one hand.

"You just relax, cowboy, and let me do the work."

When she'd worked the gel into a thick lather she began spreading it over his body. First his arms and the hollow spots beneath them. Then his chest, swirling the bubbles around his nipples, pinching them lightly. With careful strokes she rubbed the gel into the line of hair arrowing down to his groin. When she closed her hands over his rigid cock a low moan rumbled from his throat.

"Holy god, sweetheart. Careful or this will be over before it starts."

"Don't you worry about a thing," she grinned. "I've got it all in hand."

He laughed. "I'd say so."

She soaped his erection from root to tip and back again, then massaged lather into the heavy sac between his thighs. When she'd covered every inch of his legs, she nudged him to turn around and went to work on his back, beginning with his shoulders and working her way down.

When she reached the cleft of his buttocks and slid her soapy fingers into it, his muscles tightened in response.

"You know what that does to me," he reminded her.

"Exactly," and she continued massaging the gel into his flesh, probing the tight ring of his anus, penetrating it with just the tip of her finger.

By the time she'd finished lathering every inch of him and rinsing him off, she knew he was hotter than a match and ready to flare. Just the way she wanted him.

She didn't even dry them off, just stepped into the bubbling water of the hot tub and held out her hand to him. The tip of her tongue wet her lips as her eyes swept over every powerful masculine inch of him. Tonight she was in control and she would relish every minute of it.

When they were submerged to their shoulders, facing each other, she scooted between his wide-spread legs, running her hands over his muscular thighs and up the insides to the heavy sac below his cock. With a teasing touch she ran her fingertips over the soft skin, cupping his balls and rolling them in her fingers.

"Don't move," she told him. "This is my show."

She watched his muscles tighten with sexual tension and heat flare in his eyes. From the first day they'd met the fire between them had never lessened. She hadn't thought it was possible for their sexual activities to get better but he was always inventive, always thinking of new ways to bring her to climax. Tonight it was her turn to pleasure him.

Wrapping the fingers of her other hand around his stiff shaft, she moved both hands in cadence, feeling him pulse in her grip.

"Would you like to touch me?" she asked, an impish tone in her voice.

"You know damn well I would," he growled.

"All right. You may play with my nipples."

She hitched even closer to give him easier access to her. When his fingers gripped her hardened tips and pulled and tugged on them, she slid the hand toying with his balls even lower. The water was up to her chin as her fingers crept into the crevice of his ass and searched for the puckered skin of his anus. She'd discovered how much he loved this, although he'd been embarrassed to admit it the first time they experimented. Now, sometimes, she even made him beg for it. But not tonight. Tonight it was all about him.

The muscles of his buttocks clenched when she probed at him with a fingertip and his breath hissed between his teeth.

"Holy god," he growled. "You're driving me crazy."

"That's the idea," she grinned.

He rocked back and forth on the dual stimulation. As her hand moved more rapidly on his cock, her finger slid incrementally into his ass, rubbing the sensitive tissues as she explored farther and farther. With the water bubbling softly around them and the blend of aromas floating in the room, she adjusted her position to allow her the greatest access to his rectum.

Faster and faster her hand moved, up and down, her slender finger fucking his ass in time to her movements. His fingers tightened on her nipples, squeezing them hard, and she knew he was close. She pushed her finger deeper inside him to find that spot that she knew drove him over the edge. She could see it in his eyes, feel it in the tension of his body.

"Now," she whispered.

His balls tightened against her thighs and the throbbing of his cock increased.

"Happy anniversary, sweetheart," she murmured. "Let it go. Come for me now."

He exploded, the muscles in his neck cording, his head thrown back, and beneath the scented bubbles his semen spurted over and over onto her stroking hand and fingers.

"Grace!" he yelled. "Grace. Grace. Grace."

* * * * *

"Grace. Damn it, Grace, do you hear me?"

Grace shook her head, hearing Melanie's voice rather than her sexy cowboy's. He wasn't the one calling her name. Where had he gone?

"Can you hear me, Grace?" Melanie demanded. "Are you all right? You've been standing here staring into space as if you were in another world. What is the matter with you?"

Heat flooded Grace's face. The poster had thrown her into an erotic daydream right here in broad daylight, blanking out everything else. How long had she been standing here like this? What had people going back and forth in the hallway thought of her?

Without thinking she lifted her hand and touched the pin, feeling it warm against her skin. Maybe that woman was right about it. Was that a good thing or a bad one?

"Sorry." She let out a breath. "I guess my mind just wandered for a minute."

Melanie looked at the poster on the wall and back at Grace. A slow smile tilted the corners of her mouth. "Well, no wonder. Want to meet him in person? Or at least the closest thing to him?"

Grace adjusted her hat and hitched her purse strap up on her shoulder. "I'm fine, Mel. Just fine. I don't need to meet anyone. Let's go."

But Melanie just kept grinning at her. "Now that's where you're wrong. We didn't come here so you could hide in your usual corner. Let's go see if we can get you laid somewhere except in your mind."

"Wait. Wait. Are you crazy? I just—"

Melanie had a grip on Grace's arm like a vise and was practically dragging her into the huge barn that had been converted into the modern version of a chuck wagon for the rodeo contestants and workers.

"Uh-huh. Right. Forget it. I know the right cowboy is just waiting in here for you."

Oh shit. I am in such big trouble.

Chapter Two

ဆ

The big room seemed even noisier than usual, a raucous babble of voices and laughter and shouts as people recognized and greeted each other. This was opening night, so there were more people in here than usual. The long picnic tables were jammed with riders and workers catching a quick snack before getting back to business and family and friends spending a few minutes with them. No one was dressed yet for the evening's events. The rodeo would open at seven, just a couple of hours from now, and there was a lot to do before then. For everyone.

Ben Lowell leaned against a wall cradling the Styrofoam coffee cup and let his eyes travel over the gathering of people. Many of them he knew—fellow competitors, rodeo workers, ranch hands bringing the stock specially raised for rodeo competition or delivering horses newly trained for their events. Ben had ridden those "special" bulls for years and had the scars to prove it. His cutting horse, a big Appaloosa named Hotshot, had come from one of the largest ranches in Texas whose trailers were parked all over the lots here at the rodeo grounds.

And of course there were the usual buckle bunnies, the rodeo groupies who chased after every competitor. They were easily recognized in their glitzy Western wear, heavy makeup and blatant sexual smiles. Ben had been doing this for what seemed like forever, racking up an impressive list of wins, but lately he'd been feeling much older than his thirty-two years. He hated to admit how many "bunnies" he'd shared time with but now even that was getting old. He was ready for a change in his life but he had no idea what that would be.

He was sipping his coffee, not really focusing on anyone or anything, when she came into the room and he almost dropped his cup. The first thing he wondered was what she was doing here. She certainly didn't look like a rodeo hound, although the same couldn't be said of the woman with her. No, this one had a freshness about her, almost an invisible glow. Her clothes were obviously new, probably purchased for her outing. Even the hat sitting atop her chin-length warm brown hair probably came from one of the vendors here.

He knew the woman she was with. Everyone knew Melanie Keyes, most of them much better than Ben did except by reputation. She'd put it out there in Fort Worth one night, letting him know she was available, but she hadn't even made his cock tingle. Since then, whenever they'd run into each other, she gave him a look that would make ice feel warm

Now Melanie was waving at everyone as she made her way through the room, tugging the newbie behind her. When they were close enough for him to get a better look, Ben realized the woman was not as young as he'd first thought. Her face was a curious mixture of innocence and maturity, as if she'd seen a lot of life but hadn't really lived it. Not a hard look though, he told himself. Not at all.

The new clothes were little disguise for a lush figure with ripe curves. Curves a man could hold onto.

This is a woman I could sink into and stay forever.

Now where the hell had that come from? He wasn't scoping out the scene for another casual fuck. Far from it. He'd made up his mind to hang up his bedroom spurs for a while, figuring there was something wrong with him when none of the women fawning over him turned him on.

But this woman. Jesus! He was swamped by a desire to strip her naked, suck her breasts, taste every inch of her skin before licking her essence from what he was sure was a delicious cunt. And then plunge himself into that pussy and fuck her until neither of them knew their names. Or cared. What would she think if a stranger came up to her and said,

"Pardon me, ma'am, but I'd dearly love to fuck your brains out."

Watching her, his mind took a little side trip.

* * * * *

"I wanted you the minute I saw you." His hand shook slightly as he cupped her chin.

She lowered her eyelids, her lashes sweeping across her cheeks. "I wanted you even before I saw you." Then she clapped a hand across her mouth, as if the words had escaped the leash she had on them.

He grinned. "Before you saw me? That's a neat trick. Care to explain it to me?"

She shook her head. "Maybe later," she said in a soft voice.

He tilted her face up, forcing her to look at him. "You look so delicious my mouth's watering. I have to taste you."

When his lips brushed against the softness of her mouth, the brief contact shot arrows of desire through him, startling him. It had been a long time since a woman aroused him so easily and quickly. Or even interested him. He nibbled at her lower lip, scraping his teeth lightly against the velvety skin.

His tongue traced the seam of her lips. When they parted slightly he thrust his tongue inside, reveling in the flavor of her. Would her cunt taste as sweet? As delectable? Yes, he was sure of it. While he drank of her, his hands tugged at the snaps of her western-cut shirt, pulling the fabric apart to expose full, creamy breasts enclosed in pale lilac silk and lace. Tearing his mouth from hers, he lowered his head and licked the upper slope of her breasts, cupping them in his large palms as his thumbs rasped across nipples already hard and swollen.

She moaned and it was all he could do not to rip off the rest of her clothes and spread her legs…

* * * * *

Ben jerked his hand as hot coffee sloshed over his fingers. Shaking off the liquid, he cursed his mental ramblings, His cock hardened and swelled to the point he had to turn away before someone noticed what was happening to him. Cowboys were a randy, rowdy bunch who loved to make raunchy comments.

What in the hell was this woman doing with Melanie? They didn't look as if they had one thing in common. For sure she wasn't on the prowl.

They paused two tables away from where he was standing. Melanie threw her arms around Ross Lattimer and hugged him enthusiastically. Ben knew Ross collected buckle bunnies like some people collect pennies and it looked like he had a standing relationship with this one.

The brunette stood slightly to the side, at least as much as she could in the narrow aisles, obviously trying to distance herself from her friend's actions. She was fingering a pin on her blouse as she scanned the room, looking like she'd rather be any place else but here.

Ben had no idea what compelled him but he tossed his coffee cup in the trash barrel and worked his way over to the table.

The noise in the room was loud and distracting. Grace wanted to clap her hands over her ears, or else find a quiet place to hide but Melanie was dragging her along like a car on a towrope.

"There he is," she trilled, waving her other hand. "Ross! Hey, sweetie, here I am."

They finally made it through the crowded aisles to a lean, weathered man with light brown hair peeking out from the edges of his hat. Blue eyes looked at Melanie as if they wanted to devour her and thin lips turned up in a welcoming smile.

"Hey, Mel. About time you got her."

"Ross, this is my friend, Grace Delaney." She tugged Grace closer to her side. "This is her first rodeo. Give her a big old smack, why don't you."

Grace took a step back. She wanted to give Melanie a smack of a different kind. "That's okay. I think a handshake will do. Nice to meet you, Ross."

"Oh sweetie, come on." Melanie pulled on her again. "Unbend a little." She winked. "Ross is a great kisser."

"Maybe the lady's not into kissing strangers."

The voice was warm and deep, with a gravelly sound as if it wasn't used much. Grace turned and stared at the man next to her, nearly bumping into him and trying not to gape. The clean male scent of him made her dizzy.

Tall and lean, the black work shirt he wore matched the onyx of his eyes, which were bracketed by tiny lines. The faded jeans molded to his lean hips and muscular thighs. The black Stetson on his head was almost the same color as his raven-dark hair that hung below the collar of his shirt.

Ohmigod, she thought. *It's my cowboy.* Was it the pin again, playing tricks with her mind? With a few brush strokes he could be a dead ringer for the cowboy in the poster. Or in her book. The last scene she'd read came flooding back to her. Heat rushed straight to her core, dampening her panties with moisture and making all her nerve synapses fire at once. Was her sudden addiction to erotic romances turning her into a slut? Remembering the daydream she'd lapsed into in the corridor, she dropped her eyes, hoping he didn't notice the heat creeping up her face. My god, even Joe Delaney hadn't affected her that way.

The cowboy nodded at the man seated at the end of the bench, deliberately ignoring Melanie. "How are you, Ross?"

"Doing a damn sight better than I was a few minutes ago, now that this ray of sunshine is shining in my life again." He smacked Melanie on the butt, then pulled her onto his lap. "Mel, you know Ben Lowell, don't you?"

Grace watched Melanie's face close up.

"We've met." She turned back to Ross, who was nuzzling her neck. "Careful, sugar. We're in a public place." She clamped her hand on her hat to hold it in place as Ross continued to nibble at her.

Grace saw the cold, hard look Ben Lowell gave Melanie and wondered what that was all about. Meanwhile her friend was playing kissy-face with Ross and she herself was getting weak-kneed over a man she'd just met. She'd known this was a bad idea to begin with and wanted out of there *now*.

"Listen." She hoped she didn't sound as desperate as she felt. "Why don't I wander around the vendor booths some more while you and Ross get reacquainted? Just give me my ticket and I'll meet you in the arena."

A warm hand closed over her elbow, sending tingles of sensation rippling along her flesh. "Why don't I buy you a cup of coffee while Melanie and Ross do their thing?"

"Oh that sounds terrific, if you're sure you don't mind." Melanie's enthusiasm was hard to miss. It wasn't just a chance for Grace to meet someone. Melanie wanted to play games with Ross and set herself up for later. She dug into her purse and extracted a piece of pasteboard from her wallet, holding it out to Grace. "Here's your ticket. We'll catch up in the arena."

Ben palmed the ticket before she could grab it. "Great idea."

"But—" Grace had a feeling things were spinning out of her control.

"And Ben?" Melanie gave him a hard look. "You be real nice to my friend. You hear me? I know you've got manners hidden in there somewhere."

Grace chewed her bottom lip, trying to think of a way out of this that wouldn't be too awkward, even while her secret inner self was yelling, *Go with him, stupid.*

"That's okay." She would have backed away if the aisle between the tables wasn't so jammed. "Just give me the ticket. I can keep myself busy."

But Ben Lowell was already steering her away and suddenly she found herself moving along with him as if it were the most natural thing in the world. They found a picnic table in a far corner of the room that was surprisingly nearly empty and he settled her on the bench.

"I know I said coffee," he told her, "but the stuff they serve here isn't much good except as a varnish remover. How about a cold drink? Or a beer?"

Grace wet her lips nervously. "A cold drink would be fine. Anything. I'm not choosy."

She watched him walk up to one of the food counters with a loose, swivel-hipped walk she'd seen on cowboys on television and in the movies. Unconsciously she rubbed the pin, which seemed to heat her skin right through her shirt, wondering if the woman had been right and it was directing the course of her life. Melanie had hit the nail on the head about one thing. That course definitely needed changing.

"Here you go." Ben set two tall cups of soda on the table then sat down across from her.

"Thank you." She forced herself to look up at him. "We haven't actually been introduced." She held out her hand. "I'm Grace Delaney."

He took her small hand in his larger one and the touch of his flesh against hers sent the lust spiking higher. Good god. It had to be the damn pin. Maybe she should take it off before she did something embarrassing. Like throw herself at this man.

No, not me. Pin or not, that takes more courage than I have at the moment.

"Hello, Grace Delaney. I'm Ben Lowell."

"I got that much." He was still holding her hand and strangely, she had no desire to pull it away.

"I guess I just sort of took things for granted back there," he told her somewhat apologetically, "but it looked like you weren't too anxious to hang around Melanie and Ross."

"She's an old friend," she told him, wondering how well Ben knew her.

He looked at her over the rim of his cup. "I hope you don't mind my saying this and no offense intended but you and Melanie don't exactly seem like you'd have a lot in common."

"You're right but we've known each other most of our lives." She saw the tightening of his lips. "Believe me, I know exactly who and what she is but it doesn't matter. She's always been there when I needed her. That's what counts."

He glanced across the room at the woman in question. "I guess sometimes strange friendships are the best ones."

Now that she was actually looking at her dream man in the flesh, Grace felt a bad case of nerves clutch at her along with the most consuming flash of lust she could ever remember having. She took a sip of her drink to steady herself.

"So. Are you competing in the rodeo?"

His mouth thinned for a moment then he nodded briefly. "You'd think I'd have enough sense at my age to keep from getting knocked around anymore."

"I guess it wouldn't be polite to ask how old you are." Shivers rocketed through her as his thumb caressed her knuckles.

"Thirty-two going on fifty." His smile didn't quite reach his eyes.

"Pretty young," she teased, then wondered why she'd said such a stupid thing.

"Oh?" One eyebrow lifted. "I sure don't feel that young. Would it be too rude if I asked how old *you* are?"

She tried to pull her hand back but he held onto it firmly.

"Come on," he coaxed. "Tit for tat."

Squirming on the bench she said, "F-Forty-four."

"Just the right age," he said in a soft voice.

"For what?" Then she flapped a hand. "Never mind. Anyway, thanks for the rescue."

One corner of his mouth lifted in a half grin. "No problem. You looked a little desperate."

She knew she was blushing. "Sorry. You'd think I never got out of the house, wouldn't you?"

"Do you?" he teased. "Get out of the house, that is?"

Grace sighed and took another swallow of her drink. "Yes but not so you'd know it, I guess."

"Is there a Mr. Delaney?"

"Not for the last twenty years." She waited for the stab of pain that usually accompanied acknowledgement of Joe's death but somewhere in the past two decades it had disappeared. How had she not noticed? "He…passed away."

"I'm sorry. Pardon me while I take my foot out of my mouth."

"No, that's all right." She waved a hand at him. "It's a normal question."

"Any children?" he asked.

"Two and they're both out of the house and on their own, so it's just me." She shook herself. "Oh lord. I sound too pathetic for words."

Ben smiled at her. "Not at all. I'd say you had a pretty demanding life if you raised the kids yourself. And I'm guessing you worked?"

"Yes. I started out doing freelance bookkeeping at home while I got my accounting degree. Now I have my own business." She dropped her eyes, unexpectedly embarrassed, wondering what he thought of a dowdy little accountant.

"I'd say you did pretty damn good for yourself. What do you call your business?"

"Delaney Accounting Services." She made herself laugh. "Couldn't get much more boring than that, right?"

"Well, Grace Delaney, I have the feeling that you're probably anything *but* boring."

His fingers on her skin, the warm sound of his voice made her pulse leap and strange feelings cartwheel through her.

With her free hand Grace lifted her cup and drank some of her soda, trying to cool her heated emotions. "But enough about me. Your turn. Is there a Mrs. Lowell?"

"No. Like you I'm unattached." His eyes seemed to stare right into her. "Isn't that convenient."

Grace couldn't have said what they talked about for the next hour. She simply let herself be carried away by the sound of Ben's deep voice and the erotic images of him naked that kept dancing in her head. She looked around the room once and realized Melanie and Ross had taken themselves off but that was the only thing that registered on her consciousness.

I really must be losing my mind.

She vaguely remembered Ben telling her he had to get ready for the opening of the evening's program, giving her the ticket and directions to the arena.

"So." He picked up her hand again. "Can I talk you into meeting me at nine thirty when I'm through?"

He was doing that thing with his fingers again, sending electric flashes along her arm. For a moment she couldn't breathe. Go off with him? Alone? Just the two of them?

"Just drinks and dinner," he added, as if sensing her uncertainty. Then he gave her his slow, sexy smile. "And of course, anything else we might both choose to do."

She knew exactly what he was saying. She was so far out of practice with anything like this she didn't know if she was supposed to play coy, hard to get, or what. She knew only that uncharacteristically she had a burning lust for this man that had zapped her from nowhere. If she made a fool of herself, at least no one else would know.

"I came with Melanie. If I stay I won't have a way home."

"You won't have to worry about that. I promise you. Tell you what." He rose from the chair, bringing her with him. "I have to go. You think about it and if the answer is yes, you'll be waiting for me at the work exit at the rear of the arena. If not?" He shrugged. "We can think about what might have been." He lifted her hand and kissed it. "But I hope you'll be there. Take care, sugar."

She watched him walk away with that loose, swivel-hipped walk before dropping back into her chair because she wasn't sure her legs would support her.

Could she do it? Go meet a man twelve years younger than she was? With sex the uppermost thing in both of their minds? Oh god, was she crazy? But her body was rapidly winning the battle with her common sense. She was so aroused her nipples were like hard points thrusting against the soft fabric of her new shirt and she didn't think her panties could get much wetter.

Sighing, she reached up and rubbed the little pin on her collar. Was it sending her messages? Was that what the heat was all about?

Finishing her drink, she picked up both empty cups and carried them to a trash can, then looked at her watch. She had exactly three hours to decide if she was bold enough to take the next step to an adventure.

Chapter Three

ଛ

Grace took off her cowboy hat, ran her fingers through her hair to fluff it out and placed the hat back on her head for the fourth time, then looked at her watch again. Nine thirty-one. Thirty seconds later than the last time she'd sneaked a peek. The wide roadway between the back of the arena and the barns was filled with the ebb and flow of the crowd and the chaos of shouting voices. She felt like a fish out of water, flopping around seeking a familiar environment.

She'd just about decided to see if someone at the main gate could call a cab for her when the door opened and Ben strode out. He was still dressed in the brown twill pants and embroidered Western shirt he'd worn for his events and the aroma of animal and dust still clung to him but to Grace it was a heady perfume.

"Sorry." He closed his fingers over her elbow and started leading her toward a parking lot at the end of the roadway. "Sometimes it's hard to break away. Everyone wants to talk."

"I can understand why." She settled the strap of her purse more securely on her shoulder. "You won both of your events. Everyone wants to congratulate a winner."

"So what did you think of my ride?"

She gave him a small grin. "Not bad. Not bad at all."

She had, in fact, loved it. The air was charged with excitement as the bull riders came out of the chute, each massive animal doing his best to dislodge his rider. Adrenaline surged through her as if she herself was mounted on the furious animal and her heart pounded in cadence with the screams of the crowd. Leather, animal and sweat tickled her nose like a potent aphrodisiac and impossibly, she found her crotch soaked even more as her feminine juices released in response to the stimulation. Who knew that blistering hot cowboys and the ambience of the rodeo would elicit a greater sexual response from her than the few men she'd spent time with in recent years?

"So which event was your favorite?" he asked.

"I liked the calf roping but I thought my heart would stop when I saw you on that bull. God, Ben. It was like being on there with you."

His chuckle held little amusement. "I think my heart was beating right along there with yours. Might be time for me to find a less dangerous line of work." He steered her to a black dual cab pickup, dug his keys out of his pocket and pressed the remote to open the door. "Here we are. Watch your step. It's a long way up."

When his hand rested on her hip to guide her into the cab, Grace thought the heat would burn the imprint of it into her skin.

Does he feel this as intensely as I do?

Don't go there, Grace. At the very most you're just a good time for one night to him. And that's about all you can handle. Have dinner, some drinks. Maybe let him coax you into bed. And don't make a fool of yourself.

She buckled her seat belt and leaned back in the embrace of the leather seat. The truck was a reflection of him—big, dark, weathered, with the same intensity that beckoned to hidden desires. The leather was butter-soft wherever she touched it and the engine purred like a well-fed cat.

"I'm guessing Melanie had some snappy little comments to make when you told her not to wait for you," he commented, as he headed the big truck toward the exit gate.

"Actually, I think she was just as happy to get rid of me. I don't doubt that she and Ross have their own plans." She pinched the top of her purse with her fingers and a self-conscious laugh whooshed up from her throat. "Anyway, she thinks I need to loosen up a little."

"I'm sure she does. No offense, Grace, and nothing about you."

Grace slid a glance at him. "You don't like her, do you." A statement, not a question.

"Let's just say I think Melanie's a little too old to be acting like she's twenty and playing musical beds."

"Oh." *So what does that say about me?*

Ben reached a hand over and squeezed her thigh. "That has absolutely nothing to do with you, darlin'. I just don't like Melanie's style and let's leave it at that."

Grace chose her words carefully. "I suppose you get a lot of older women throwing themselves at you. Rodeo hounds, you know."

Ben's hand on her thigh tightened reflexively. "Actually, they're called buckle bunnies and if you think I'm lumping you in with everyone else you can forget that right now." They were stopped at a traffic light and he turned his head to look at her. "The thing is, Grace, what attracted me to you is the fact you're so different from the usual women I…run into."

"I guess that's a good thing?" The butterflies she'd been fighting since the afternoon had decided to take full flight in her stomach. Why couldn't she get a grip on her nerves?

"You bet it is, sugar. You just bet it is."

Grace hadn't paid much attention to where they were heading but now she saw them pull into the parking area of a brand new three-story motel on the interstate frontage road.

"Um, is this where we're having dinner?"

Ben parked the truck and turned to smile at her. "Maybe. Or not. This is where I'm showering before I let myself get closer to you than I am now. I stink of rodeo. Shower first, then dinner and drinks. Okay?"

Grace nodded, gripping her purse and trying not to act like a nervous virgin. "Fine. That's fine."

She looked every place but at him as they rode up in the elevator and when he unlocked the door to his room she had to force herself over the threshold. She nervously scanned the area, noticing it was a suite, not a single room. Apparently he took good care of himself on the road.

Ben dropped his keycard and hat on a round table by the window. He took her hat off and tossed it to the table next to his and began to unbutton his shirt. Grace's fingers twitched with the urge to run through the dark curls covering his chest.

"Would you like something from the minibar to tide you over?" he asked. "Or maybe just a cold drink?"

She shook her head. "No, thanks. I'm fine."

He picked up the remote, clicked on the television and handed the control to her. "Make yourself comfortable. I'll be out pretty quick."

Grace sat gingerly in a big armchair, clutching the remote. She couldn't have said what was on the screen in front of her because her brain was processing an image of Ben stripping off his clothes in the bathroom and stepping naked into the shower. Closing her eyes, she leaned back and let her purse fall to the floor, forgetting where she was, thinking only of a naked Ben Lowell. She slid her hand between her thighs, caressing herself through the fabric of her jeans, a practice that was her release trigger when the spiral coiled too tightly. A way to satisfy herself without needing another person. Certainly none of the men she'd finally gotten around to dating lit one tiny sexual spark.

Sometimes, especially when she was reading one of her new erotic romances, her hand would steal to her warm flesh, feel the dripping moisture in her cunt and like now she'd rub her clit until she finally climaxed.

Melanie had finally talked her into buying herself some battery-operated friends but she didn't exactly carry one

33

around in her purse. Why should she? This was private, in the secrecy of her home.

Over the years she'd reached a point where suppressing her sexual urges had made her uptight and edgy but nothing had ever brought her to her current state of arousal. Just looking at Ben, listening to him, sent her hormones racing around her body at an unfamiliar speed.

Her hand moved in the familiar rhythm as she spread her thighs and gave in to the need driving her. When a large, warm hand covered hers and moved over the mound of her cunt with her she was so startled she almost stopped breathing.

"You should have joined me in the shower." Ben's gravelly voice was soft against her ear and his warm breath tickled her skin. "And here I had this big seduction scene all planned."

"Oh! My god!" Heat bloomed in her face and panic tripled her heart rate. How much more embarrassed could she be?

She tried to jerk her hand away but Ben closed his fingers over it.

"Don't be embarrassed. I like to watch a woman touch herself." He paused. "The right woman. I'll bet this would feel a lot better without all these clothes on, sugar."

"Ben, I—"

"Come on."

He tugged her up from the chair where she was sitting. That was when she realized he was wearing only a bath towel knotted at the waist.

"You're... You're not..."

He grinned at her. "I forgot to bring clean clothes into the bathroom with me. I thought I'd sneak out and get them but the image that greeted me was more than I could stand."

His warm fingers were opening first one button, then another on her shirt. He stared at the swell of her breasts for a long moment, hunger sparking in his eyes, before he lifted his hands to cup her face.

"I know you'll taste real good, Grace. Real good."

I have to get out of here. What am I thinking? Grace Delaney doesn't do this. I'm not sure I even know how. Oh god, oh god. Brain, engage and let me think.

But her brain had shut down for the night. And Ben, it seemed, was a man with a plan. Letting her pull away from him didn't seem to be part of it. His lips brushed across hers as gently as a bird's wing, pressing so lightly she wasn't even sure of the contact. The tip of his tongue traced the outline of her mouth, licking the corners and tasting the surface of her lips. His taste was like warm honey and when she opened her mouth on a soft sigh his tongue moved inside in a graceful slide.

Yes, warm honey, she thought. Then every inhibition, every defense she'd carefully built up over the years crumbled like bleu cheese. She gave herself over to the heat coursing through her as the surface of his tongue coaxed hers into a sensual dance, twisting and twining with it, while his gentle calloused hands cradled her face. Her breath was clogged in her throat and her pulse was beating like the wings of a drunken butterfly. He took the kiss so deep, tasting every inner surface of her mouth and enticing her to do the same with him, that she was sure she was drowning in it.

He tasted like mint toothpaste and smelled of soap and just like earlier in the day, his clean male scent made her senses reel. When his tongue began to retreat from her mouth she closed her teeth over it, lightly, unwilling to lose the intimate contact. He was pure sin, invading every inch of her body, and she didn't want him ever to stop kissing her like this. Not ever.

She gripped his wrists to steady herself, acutely aware of the fine, silken hair on his skin. At last he lifted his head but he didn't move away. Instead his mouth trailed across her cheek and the tip of his tongue licked the sensitive spot behind one ear, drawing feathery little circles. Shivers skipped along her spine and plucked at her skin.

His lips moved along the edge of her collarbone, nipping here and there, pausing at the hollow of her throat where her pulse was beating so hard she was afraid it would burst through the thin layer of skin. Then down, down, down to the swell of her breasts, his tongue like a flaming icicle, hot and cold, skimming across the surface.

"I want to feel your naked skin," he murmured as he slid his hands down to her shirt, her fingers still wrapped around his wrists.

Grace felt the pin almost glowing against her body through the fabric, tendrils of heat emanating straight to the hungry flesh of her cunt. She hardly realized it when Ben deftly slid his hands from her grip, finished unbuttoning her blouse and eased it down her arms. She was drifting in a fog of arousal, heading to a place she'd never been before, half lustful, half scared.

His mouth was on her again, drugging her so she didn't even feel him unclasp her bra. She was only aware of it when cool air drifted over her heated skin and his lips closed around one hard, pebbled nipple demanding to be sucked. His tongue flicked over it, then pressed it against the roof of his mouth, trapping it in his warm heat. His teeth raked gently over the beaded nub before he drew it into his mouth again, then blew a soft stream of air over the wet flesh.

She shuddered, unconsciously cupping her breasts and lifting them to him. His moan of satisfaction echoed through her, raising the level of her need even more. A piece of her brain tried to pull her back from a deep well of sensuality.

What am I doing what am I doing what am I doing?

But it was too late. Mistake or not, she couldn't have walked out the door to save her life. And she discovered, with a mixture of fear and curiosity, that she didn't want to.

Ben looked up at her, his eyes heavy-lidded and sensual, his face flushed with desire. "You have beautiful breasts, Grace. I could spend all night doing nothing but worshiping them. Your nipples look so sweet I could fall asleep with one of them in my mouth and be a happy man."

"But they… But I…"

"Are a beautiful, mature woman with a body that demands proper attention. I'm guessing that's never happened but I'm going to change that tonight."

"But…But…"

But I'm twelve years older than you.

"But nothing. You're absolutely perfect exactly as you are. Don't spoil my enjoyment listing imperfections that don't exist, okay?"

She was conscious of his hard erection poking through the fabric of the towel, the thin denim of her jeans an insubstantial barrier to the pressure against her cunt. Needing more, she pushed her hips against him and she felt him smile against her skin.

"Oh yes. We'll get to that too, sugar. But we've got all night to learn what makes each other feel good."

His fingers opened the snap on her jeans and the rasp of the zipper being lowered sounded so loud in her head. He moved so he could lower her jeans and thong to her ankles. She was momentarily embarrassed at the satisfied grin that tilted his lips when he felt how drenched the fabric of her crotch was. Then he lifted her and carried her into the bedroom. With one swift movement of his arm he yanked the covers back and guided her to sit on the edge of the mattress so he could rid her of her boots. His careful hands removed the last thing covering her and he just stood there, staring at her, his breath a raspy sound.

Grace was afraid to open her eyes, afraid of what she'd see there. Afraid the vestiges of stretch marks and the imperfections of age would, despite his words, turn him off.

But when she forced her eyes open she was shocked to see the intensity of the lust burning in his. His gaze swept over her slowly, taking in every exposed inch of her. His hands, when they reached out to touch her, were trembling slightly.

He's nervous too. Who'd have thought it?

But then she was lost in a swirl of sensation again as those hands explored the surface of her body, reading every inch of her skin, every dip and curve and crevice. She wanted him to hurry but he seemed intent on taking as long as possible, discovering what she liked, what drew little moans and gasps from her in the secret places his fingers explored.

When he reached down to her ankles to lift her legs the towel, which had been perched precariously low on his hips, lost its battle with gravity and slipped to the floor. The sight of his cock—proud, erect, magnificent, jutting thickly from curls as dense as those on his chest—stunned her. Grace's hands itched to reach out for him, to touch and explore that heavy stalk and the sac lying below it. But then Ben lifted her legs, bent them at the knees and planted her feet on the bed and the only thing important to her was the center of her heat, her cunt, where her muscles were already quivering in anticipation.

"God, Grace," he breathed. "You are every man's wet dream. Soft thighs, a tummy rounded just a little to pillow my head on and a pussy so delicious looking I want to dive in and never come up for air."

Her hands gripped the sheet as he knelt between her legs, lifted them to his shoulders and carefully parted her tender labia, covered with the liquid heat of her desire. His tongue blazed a careful trail the length of her slit, one sweep from top to bottom, then back again.

"You taste just like I thought you would." His voice was thick and husky. "Like ripe fruit."

He bent his head between her thighs again, the rough calluses on his fingers waking up the nerve endings in her labia as he peeled it open once more and began to use his tongue in earnest. The tip teased at the entrance to her vagina, circling it again and again before slipping just inside to lap at her liquid. Then back out and around and around before dipping farther into her well-lubricated channel.

Grace could hardly hold herself still, her hips bucking and thrusting as Ben's tongue moved farther inside her each time it entered her. A hot coil of need tightened in her belly then began to unwind with agonizing slowness. Everything fell away except Ben and his wickedly clever tongue.

Until he shifted one hand and rubbed his thumb back and forth against the swollen bundle of nerves that was her clitoris, the jolt of sensation stabbing through her. His tongue stiffened and plunged deeper inside her while his thumb moved with the steady rhythm of an erotic metronome. Always taking her higher. Just a little higher. But never letting her reach the place she wanted—needed—so badly. She could hardly believe the guttural moan she heard came from her own mouth and her hips pushed harder at him, silently begging him to give her release.

His hands slipped beneath the cheeks of her buttocks and pulled her tighter to his mouth, his tongue moving faster and faster, his thumb rubbing and rubbing. When he finally pushed her over the edge, lightning crackled around her and thunder boomed in her ears. Her body shuddered again and again and the muscles in her cunt spasmed with a deep, sucking pull, drawing his tongue into her as far as it would go.

Ben held her firmly as the climax shook her, his hands the only anchor in an erotic storm that swirled around her and tossed her in a darkness like black velvet.

Her breathing had barely returned to anything resembling normal when Ben moved over her, sliding her farther back on the mattress so he could lay full length on top of her, his weight supported on his forearms. He kissed her, his lips moving back and forth against hers before his tongue teased entrance into her mouth as it had with her pussy. The flavor of her essence shocked her, tart and sweet at the same

39

time. Even when she'd brought herself to climax with her own hand she'd never been bold enough to lick her fingers as the women in her books sometimes did.

Where his tongue had been bold before, now it was gentle, barely thrusting and withdrawing. As Grace dragged breath into her lungs, she opened her eyes to find Ben's eyes barely an inch away, pinpricks of light shining from the onyx depths, his thick lashes throwing spiky shadows on his cheeks. His warm breath teased at her face and one corner of his mouth hitched up in a semblance of a grin.

"You are amazing." His deep voice vibrated against her. "Totally amazing."

"You don't think..." She had to say it. "I mean, I'm sure all the women you've slept with are much younger than I am and—"

He moved one hand to cover her mouth. "Not one more word. I'm right where I want to be. Fruit that's plucked before its time is seldom juicy and often bitter, you know."

Grace couldn't help herself. She laughed. "So did I ripen long enough on the tree? Or vine? Or whatever?"

He kissed the tip of her nose. "Just right, sugar. Just right."

Chapter Four

🔊

Grace slid her hands over Ben's shoulders, loving the feel of the taut muscles beneath the firm skin. The men she'd chosen to socialize with when she'd finally come out from what Melanie called her "cave of desolation" were older than she was, in most cases not too well toned and probably far less talented in bed than Ben Lowell. That is, if she'd ever given them a chance. But none of them had pushed her hot button even a little.

"You choose safe men just like you chose a safe career," Melanie repeated over and over. "Jesus, break the mold once in a while, will you? What can you lose?"

Myself. I don't know how to handle it.

And she probably wouldn't even be here with Ben if she hadn't developed her new reading habit and with it, a healthy curiosity. If the rest of tonight was anything like the beginning, she'd gladly deal with the fallout tomorrow. Whatever it turned out to be.

"You're thinking so hard I can almost hear the wheels in your brain move," Ben teased. "Don't you know good sex is supposed to shut off your mind? Maybe I'm not doing it right."

Grace wrapped her arms around his neck and hugged him. "You're doing it just fine. It's me. I think I forgot how to let it all go."

He nipped at her ear and licked it lightly with the tip of his tongue. "You let it go just right as far as I'm concerned, darlin'. And before tonight is over, I'm going to make sure you let all the rest of it go."

41

She rubbed herself against him, the soft pelt of hair on his chest abrading lightly against her breasts, hardly able to believe how good it felt. The orgasm he had given her with his mouth was so completely unbelievable, wringing her dry, and she hadn't even felt his penis inside her yet. And oh yes, she definitely wanted to feel it. In her hands, her mouth, her vagina. All those things she'd read about so avidly.

Melanie might have been the one who literally shoved her out of the house, dressed her in strange clothes and pushed her into a foreign environment. But maybe, underneath it all, she'd been ready for this. Just reluctant to face possible failure and rejection. Maybe it was the pin, the burnished metallic boot, just like the woman had said. Maybe she finally wanted to find out what other women experienced that she never had. Whatever the reason, her cultivated reticence was giving way to a burgeoning curiosity and suddenly she wanted it all...except she wasn't quite sure what *all* meant.

Ben's mouth was at her breasts again, teeth tugging at her nipples and tongue soothing them. Quivering sensations vibrated in her pussy again and she could tell she was wet again. Wanting more than before. A lot more.

He moved his mouth over her body as if drawing a map with it, tasting every nook and crevice, seeking her pleasure spots and dwelling a long time on them. His open-mouthed kisses on her heated skin sent shafts of electricity through her, igniting nerves already snapping and firing.

His cock pressed against the soft skin of her inner thigh and her hands suddenly itched to touch it and hold it. Pulling Ben's head up from its drifting path down to her pussy, she smiled at him. "Stop."

His eyebrows raised. "Stop? Am I doing something wrong? Something you don't like? Just tell me—"

"No. You're doing everything just right. But I want to play too." She pushed at his shoulders.

"And just what is it you want to do?" he asked, his eyes bright with curiosity as he rolled onto his back.

"This."

Wondering where this spurt of boldness had come from, she shifted onto her knees next to him, her gaze riveted to his erection, which pointed directly at her. Tentatively she reached out a finger to touch the bead of fluid sitting like a viscous marble atop the slit. Rubbing it back and forth along the velvet surface, she watched the thick stalk bob under her touch and saw Ben's thigh muscles tighten.

She hadn't done this since Joe's death. The few men she'd had sex with hadn't appealed to her this way at all. Sometimes she wondered if they really appealed to her in *any* way. Worried that maybe she just wasn't a sexual person.

No. Wait. Then she wouldn't be where she was doing what she was. Right?

Inquisitively, she bent her head and licked the surface of the purple head with the tip of her tongue, swiping it back and forth two or three times, loving the slightly salty taste of the fluid and the sensation of the soft skin against her tongue. Her fingers barely wrapped around the thick length of him but she felt the steel beneath the supple covering. She unclasped him and ran one finger the length of the heavy vein, feeling the blood pulsing through it.

"Am I doing this right?" she asked, her voice tremulous, unable to look at him as she waited for his answer.

"Are you kidding?" Ben asked in a strangled voice, one large hand coming up to squeeze her buttocks. "I think you're trying to torture me."

Grace's laugh held just a hint of uncertainty. "Just finding out what you feel like. How you feel."

His hand moved in slow strokes on the cheek of her ass. "Surely this isn't the first one you've ever seen or felt," he joked.

"Believe it or not, the first in bright light. At least for longer than I want to remember."

Because the others didn't bear looking at. Except for Joe, who was so very young.

He shifted his position to lay flatter on the bed and opened his thighs. "I won't even begin to ask about the reasons for that. Just...go ahead." His voice was tight with his effort at control. "Play to your heart's content."

Grace stroked his penis in a slow up-and-down motion, loving the feel of the skin as it moved beneath her touch and the hardening of the shaft beneath it. When another bead of liquid seeped from the slit she bent and licked it away, then ran her tongue across her lips.

"Jesus, Grace." His breath whistled through her teeth. "Have mercy."

With a boldness that surprised her, she opened her mouth and slid it along his cock, pulling it into her in tiny increments until the head hit the back of her throat. Forcing back the gag reflex, she caressed the shaft with her tongue as her hand pumped the root of it where it was still exposed.

Ben hitched his hips slightly, moving with the rise and fall of her hand, his cock throbbing against the suction of her mouth.

Grace felt a sudden surge of power at the control she was exerting over this man. Her pitiful list of lovers had been more interested in their own satisfaction than attending to hers. And sex with Joe Delaney, while wonderful, had been so long ago and had yet to develop a maturity to it. Everything had been a learning process for both of them. This was a whole new world for her and the excitement of it rose like a waterfall within her.

She swirled her tongue more rapidly and pumped her hands harder, her other hand drifting to the sac that lay heavy between his legs, cradling the warmth of it in her palm. Lost in the cadence of her movements, she opened her eyes when she heard Ben groan loudly and felt his hand slide up her back to her neck. His face was flushed, his eyes closed but his mouth partly open.

As she drew her mouth along his penis up to the furled skin at the head, running the tip of her tongue through the slit, Ben's fingers tightened on her neck and he pulled her head back.

"Enough," he gasped. "When I come tonight I want it to be in your cunt, not your mouth. Not this first time."

He rolled her to the side and with a smooth, graceful movement, palmed the condom he'd dropped on the nightstand. He positioned himself between Grace's thighs, his big body nudging them farther apart. His eyes were burning with such heated lust Grace was sure one blink would set fire to them both. Bending his head for a moment, he lapped her slit, testing it for readiness.

"Wet," he whispered. "And deliciously so. Bend your knees, Grace, and spread your thighs as wide as you can."

His eyes ate at her while he hastily sheathed himself. Then he was holding his cock with one hand and separating the lips of her pussy with the other. Slowly pushing himself into her vagina. His eyes locked on hers as he filled her waiting, hungry channel. She knew she was tight and her flesh had to stretch to accommodate him but any pain was overridden by the intense pleasure rushing through her body. She was sure there wasn't an inch of her core that wasn't filled with the thickness of him.

With each deeper penetration her body opened up to him more until she wanted to scream at him to hurry, hurry, hurry. But he was just as determined to prolong the process, pulling out until only the very tip was inside her, then pushing back inside. He did it again. And again. Grace wrapped her legs around his lean hips, crossed her ankles at the small of his back and tried to hold him in place but he just laughed.

"Slow and easy does it, darlin'. I'm guessing you haven't ridden this particular horse for a long time. I plan to make it last."

He reached one hand between them, found the nub of her clitoris and moved his thumb back and forth in a lazy motion. With every brush sparks shot straight to the center of her womb and the walls of her pussy clutched at him.

The room faded away until there was just her and this glorious male animal, locked in an erotic embrace, his cock sliding in and out in such slow, measured strokes she thought she would ignite from the climbing tension. Her blood raced in her veins, pounding so hard she could feel the pressure in her ears. She couldn't seem to get enough air in her lungs as he rolled and twisted his hips and his clever thumb coaxed every bit of response from her clit.

"Please," she begged. "Oh please."

His body tightened beneath her touch, the pace of his strokes increased and with a final, hard thrust and a shout he took them both over the edge. The force of her orgasm was so powerful that every muscle in her body clenched with the spasms and shook her until she thought her heart would stop. In the hot well of her vagina, behind the thin shield of the latex, Ben's penis pumped and pumped, filling the reservoir with spurt after spurt of semen.

She couldn't tell if it was her heartbeat or his banging so hard against her chest. The sound of air being dragged with raw intensity into starved lungs echoed in the room and the artificial air cooled their sweat-slicked bodies.

It could have been five minutes or an hour before Ben pushed himself up on his forearms and slid gently from her body, her inner muscles protesting the loss of the thick shaft they'd grasped so tightly. He moved carefully off the bed, his feet barely whispering over the carpet as he made his way to the bathroom to dispose of the condom. Grace closed her eyes, boneless in the aftermath of such complete satisfaction.

But if she thought Ben was finished with her, she was completely mistaken. Warm lips pressed a light kiss to her mouth and large, calloused hands slid beneath her body, lifting her as if she were totally weightless.

"Shower time," Ben murmured in her ear and carried her toward the bathroom.

He couldn't believe how good it felt just to hold her. Her skin was like the finest satin, so smooth to his touch he wanted to stroke it forever. He'd had to tear himself away from her breasts, warm pillows that a man could fall asleep on. Her thighs were so lush he could sink into them forever. And her cunt. Oh Jesus. Tight and wet and gripping him like a hot fist. It took every ounce of control to hang onto his climax until she was ready.

Her anxiety was so evident he'd wanted to just cradle her in his arms and tell her not to worry. She needed to be eased into this, coaxed, gently led step-by-step. His brain knew it but his body didn't. The sight of her naked body took his breath away. His brain took complete leave and all he could think of was tasting every corner of her body and finally being inside her.

And hadn't *that* been the most glorious experience. Holy Christ. She tasted like every kind of sin and pleasure in the world and felt like it too.

How could he find the best way to tell her that the women he'd been having disconnected sex with — and that was all it was these days — had starved themselves and over-exercised to where they were nothing but hard muscle and bones. It was like taking a piece of stone to bed and worrying all the time if one push would break every bone in your body or cut into your skin. Grace was like a sexy cloud, ripe and mature with the right curves.

Her age never entered the equation, not as far as he was concerned. After the past few years he felt older and far more used up than her forty-four years. Besides that, there was something so fresh and appealing about her, something that chiseled at the stone where his heart lay.

Sex with her was like nothing else he'd ever experienced. Glorious. Fulfilling. For the first time in as long as he could remember, he actually lost himself in the act and it was so much more than he'd hoped for. All he'd wanted was one night with her but now he knew it wouldn't be close to enough. The list of things he wanted to do to her — with her — unreeled endlessly in his mind. The trick would be to convince her.

And to find out how hard and how far he could push her.

At least for the time he was here. He'd make that perfectly clear. But Jesus, he wanted her in his bed every one of those nights.

He turned on the water in the shower enclosure, waited until it had reached the right temperature, then stepped inside, still holding Grace. Her head was leaning on his shoulder, her eyes closed and he wondered if she'd fallen asleep. But when he set her on her feet, her eyes opened and a sly smile quirked at her mouth.

"Is this where I get to wash your body?"

"Uh-uh, darlin'. This is where *I* get to rub lather all over *yours*, paying careful attention to all the tempting crevices."

"No fair," she told him. "I want to have fun too."

"Oh trust me." He licked the edges of her mouth then sipped gently from her shower-misted lips. "You'll have plenty of that. I promise you."

He turned her slowly beneath the soft spray until her skin glistened with drops of water, then took the soap and worked up a thick lather with his hands.

"Don't move," he commanded. "Just enjoy."

He took his time working the lather into her skin, starting with her shoulders then moving down her arms to her wrists. When he locked his soapy fingers with hers a strange feeling danced through him, one he did *not* want to identify. *Sex*, he told himself. *I want to have sex with this woman again and again. Sex. Just sex.* Anything else would open a gate to a road he'd ridden before and still had the scars to prove it.

Her skin was soft and supple, not hard and overused like most of the women he'd taken to his bed. It rippled beneath his touch like the finest silk. Her hips flared out from the indentation of her waist like a lush goddess, her thighs firm and full. Even her ankles and knees were tempting and exciting.

He nearly lost his concentration when he applied the lather to the rounded cheeks of her ass, trailing his fingers through the cleft and pausing just for an instant at the tiny opening of her anus. God, how he'd love to fuck her there. To plunge his cock into that hot, dark tunnel and ride her until she screamed her completion. He wondered if anyone had ever breached that opening or if he could be the first. If she'd let him. His cock hardened at the images that conjured up in his mind.

"Turn around," he told her in a thick voice.

Leaning her against the shower wall, he began the application of soapy lather on the front of her body, massaging it into her full breasts, tweaking the nipples and playfully dabbing bubbles on each. He tormented himself by crouching down and going directly to her ankles, bypassing her cunt although it beckoned him like a seductive drug. When he reached the tops of her thighs and ran his thumbs along the crease where hip and thigh joined, her breathing hitched and she widened her stance in silent urging.

When he plunged his soapy fingers between her folds, the walls of her vagina clamped down on him, pulling at him, and he felt them fluttering.

Jesus. This was the most responsive woman he'd ever met. Nothing was calculated or planned. She just...was. Despite the massive orgasms they'd just shared, she was riding the curve of ecstasy again, the flutters growing harder and

49

faster. A tiny moan whispered over her lips as she squeezed her thighs around his wrist.

He was surprised when she grabbed his hand and jerked it away.

"My turn." Her voice was breathless. "Stand still and don't move."

It was difficult to do as she ran her delicate fingers over his body, rubbing here, teasing there, dragging her nails over his hard nipples and down through the hair to his groin. When she lathered his rigid, ready cock, paying special attention to the head and the slit, he had to bite his tongue to retain some semblance of control. But when she reached between his legs to cup his balls, manipulating them with her fingers, he pulled away, moving her to the side.

"That's it," he groaned.

Opening the shower door, he reached for the condom he'd dropped onto the vanity, ripped open the foil and rolled it onto his erection in record time. With the strength that he'd acquired fighting the massive bulls, he lifted Grace as if she weighed nothing and impaled her on his penis, filling her with one hard, quick thrust.

"Wrap your legs around me," he commanded.

She slid them up his hips and locked her ankles at the small of his back, pulling him tight against her. Pressing her to the wall, he slammed in and out of her as if his life depended on it. His head dropped enough for him to take one rosy nipple into his mouth, sucking it hard and pressing it against the roof of his mouth before clamping it between his teeth.

Back and forth his hips pistoned. She met him thrust for thrust, a high, keening sound rising from her throat, her hands clutching his shoulders to keep her balance. He felt the orgasm rising within him, sending lightning streaks along his spine and tightening his balls.

Feeling her pulse around him, he took them both over the edge, the slick walls of her cunt pulling at him and milking him through the thin latex. He took her mouth in a totally carnal kiss, sucking her tongue into his own mouth and devouring it, licking her inner walls and drinking the nectar he found there. She never shrank from him, giving back as good as she got, riding the whirlwind with him until the very last of the aftershocks dissipated and they were limp against the shower wall.

With a hand that shook slightly, he reached over and shut off the water that had now turned cool. Lifting her onto the thick bath mat, he grabbed towels from the counter and wrapped one around each of them, carefully drying her off before carrying her back into the bedroom.

Somehow he managed to get them under the covers and pulled her next to him, spoon fashion, before dragging sheet and blanket up to their chins. His last thought before he fell into a deep sleep was that he wasn't about to let her disappear come morning. He'd find a way to convince her to stay with him until the end of the rodeo.

That was all. He'd be sure she understood—just until the end of the rodeo. Grace Delaney was definitely no buckle bunny. She was all woman and all class. But his future was too murky and he didn't want to have a mess to deal with when he moved on. Which he would do for sure.

Yup. He'd be real clear on that point.

Chapter Five

❧

Grace shoved a stack of folders aside on her desk and turned back to her computer. All morning she'd tried to force her mind to focus on financial projections and capital amortization but they might as well have been words plucked from a foreign alphabet. Financial statements, both hard copy and on her monitor screen, swam before her like waterlogged pages.

Waterlogged!

Don't go there, Grace.

But the word called up the images of that shower with Ben, steam hissing around them as they soaped each other with rich lather, the feel of his fingers inside her. Then the hard thrust as he speared her on his more-than-ready cock and rode her over the edge of a cliff to a thundering orgasm. Her panties dampened even as the thoughts raced unrestrained through her head.

How on earth had she let herself fall into such an ocean of eroticism? She, the most proper person in the world. The widow who guarded her chastity years after her husband's death. Who only learned about erotic love from the books she read and her secret DVDs. *Oh. My. God.* Ben Lowell probably thought she was the tramp of the century. As well he should. The things she'd done with him. To him. Let *him* do to *her*. *Oh. My. God.*

Despite the fact that her body felt well and thoroughly satisfied, that satisfaction was mixed with trepidation and anxiety. She simply had to get a grip on herself again, that's all there was to it.

"Mrs. Delaney?"

She looked up, shaken from her reverie. Joyce Ritter, her secretary, stood in the doorway.

Grace stared at her, confused. Why hadn't she buzzed like she usually did? Was something wrong? "Yes?" she said, puzzled.

"Are you okay?"

Grace sat up straighter in her chair and, without thinking, rubbed the little boot pin she'd fastened to her collar this morning.

"I'm fine, Joyce. Maybe just a little distracted what with quarterly statements due. Why?"

Joyce frowned at her. "I buzzed you three times and you didn't answer. Mrs. Keyes is here and says she's going to break your door down if I don't let her in."

Grace laughed, especially seeing the knowing grin on Joyce's face. Melanie was a legend with the staff. "Let her in. I need a break anyway."

The words were barely out of her mouth before Melanie swept into the room, today dressed in skintight, hand-painted, maroon jeans and a hot pink sweater. She poured herself a coffee from the carafe on the credenza, arranged herself on the couch and said, "Okay, shoot."

Grace swallowed a smile and arched an eyebrow. "Give. Are you soliciting for one of your multiple causes?"

Melanie made a rude noise. "I want to know about last night, m'dear. Details. All of them."

Grace knew she was blushing and she ducked her head toward her own coffee mug. "You know I never kiss and tell."

Melanie recrossed her legs. "Sure but that's because for the past twenty years you haven't had anything to tell *about*. Come on. I was the one who dressed you up and dragged you there. I *deserve* to know what happened."

"I got the feeling that you and Ben know each other," Grace said, changing the subject.

Melanie's smile barely faltered. "We've met. That's all."

"But there seemed to be something...oh, I don't know...maybe hostile between you?"

Melanie set her mug down on the end table. "Ben Lowell is a huge hunk of man, Grace Delaney. He's very particular these days about who he chooses to spend his time with. So if he chose you, you damn well better know I want to hear *everything*."

Was that a little venom Grace heard? She certainly didn't think there was any need for it. Regardless of what might be or have been between the two of them, there didn't seem to be anything now. Besides, she'd only been an adventure to Ben, just as he was to her. He'd given her a night she could pull out and relive lying alone in her bed, with her erotic romance novels and her battery-operated friend as enhancements. She was a realist and she knew what the score was. She was a novelty to him. Tonight he'd be moving on to someone else.

Before Grace could answer, however, the intercom sounded. "There's a phone call for you, Mrs. Delaney," her secretary's voice said. "It's a man and if you don't want him can I have him? He sounds hot."

Grace knew at once who it was, her tummy doing a tango and heat creeping up her cheeks. "He's seventy years old, Joyce," she joked.

"Yeah, right. Shall I put him through?"

The phone on her desk rang, she picked it up and the minute she heard his voice memories from the night before flooded her brain. She turned away from Melanie in case every one of her thoughts was written on her face.

"Morning, gorgeous." His voice had an early morning huskiness to it, deep and warm like fresh coffee.

"Good morning." Her mind was skittering around, trying to figure out how to talk to him with Melanie avidly eavesdropping. She turned to her friend and made a shooing motion with her hand but Melanie just grinned and shook her head. Grace dropped her voice. "I'm not alone."

"No problem. I just wanted to see if you were doing okay today. And tell you I want to see you again tonight."

See her again? No way. Not when she'd just been steeling herself for him to move on. Anyway, one night was all she could handle. She just needed the right words to tell him this wasn't her style. And it wasn't. Was it?

"Oh. Well." She bit her lip. She wondered how to get her message across with Melanie so close at hand. The clipped answers would have to do. Then she blurted out absolutely the wrong answer. "Sure."

Sure? Grace, are you nuts?

But she couldn't take it back with Melanie sure to ask questions.

"Great." Was that a sigh of relief she heard? "We can talk more when no one's around. Want to see the rodeo again? I'm competing again tonight."

"Yes, please. I think I'd like that." *Okay, that's safe. See the rodeo, get the hell out of there.*

Yeah, right.

"All right then." She could hear the grin in his voice. "How about taking a cab so you won't have to worry about your car? I'll have a VIP pass waiting for you at the main gate."

"But—" *Not have my own car? How will I get home? Can I leave myself without that security?*

"No buts. I'll drive you home in the morning and I don't want any arguments about it. Other ears are listening, remember?" he teased. "Meet me at the back door at nine thirty. See you tonight, darlin'."

Before she could say anything else, he'd hung up.

In the morning? Drive her home in the morning? How was she going to get herself out of this one? Did she even want to?

Fast. So fast. Too much too fast. For a moment she almost couldn't catch her breath.

"Well!" Melanie stood up. "I'm sure I don't have to ask who that was, even though you did your damndest to hide it. Seeing him again? Good for you." She kissed Grace on the cheek. "Remember, I'll be waiting for those details."

Grace sat at her desk, staring into space, Ben's naked body the only thing she could think of, until Joyce buzzed her that a client was waiting to see her.

* * * * *

Sitting through an hour with Leo Dandridge had been slow torture, not to mention reviewing two reports one of her part-timers had prepared. Somehow the safe world of accounting didn't hold Grace's attention today.

At least a dozen times she lifted the phone to call Ben's hotel and leave a message for him. No, that would be rude, she argued with herself. Besides, she was no coward. Was she? She could tell him in person that this couldn't go on.

Of course, she told herself, it wouldn't hurt to look and feel terrific when she gave him her speech. It would give her confidence. Right. Confidence.

Who am I kidding? That was just a taste. I want to know it all. Every bit of it. To find myself as a woman.

Only Ben Lowell might just be a lot more than she could handle.

At home she treated herself to a long bubble bath then rubbed lavender lotion onto every inch of her body. From her lingerie drawer she pulled out the sheer lace red thong and matching demi-bra, eyeing herself in the mirror critically after she'd put them on. Maybe Ben overlooked the stretch marks but to her they looked like vivid silver streaks, as did the matching ones on the undersides of her breasts. Or maybe they were just more obvious to her.

Well, nothing she could do about them now.

The rest of her body was passable. Ben seemed happy with it, so she guessed that was all that counted.

He spoke of "exploring". What kinds of things did he mean? She knew that sexually she was — what? Not repressed but certainly uninitiated. There was so much she didn't know. Hadn't experienced. Wondered if she even *wanted* to experience. At her age did she even have the right to want something that pushed the boundaries? How far would Ben take this? And how far would she be willing to go?

Listen, Grace, one more night won't kill you. It's not as if the guy lives here or anything. It can be your little secret.

One night, she reminded herself. And then I'll give him "the speech".

Half of her closet was on the floor by the time she decided on navy slacks and a red silk blouse, with the pin sitting on the collar. She ran her fingers over it, feeling heat emanate from it as if it were a living thing. Help her find her lover, huh? Not that she believed in myths and legends but she'd met Ben right after that, so who knew what else was in store.

Gritting her teeth against the pinch of the new boots as she slipped them on, she placed the new hat firmly on her head and hurried out to the waiting cab.

* * * * *

The rodeo was just as exciting the second night, the animals as magnificent, the contestants brilliant in their execution. And again the mingled scents of the rodeo teased at her senses, making her blood rush in her veins. Grace's adrenaline was flowing on high when Ben came through the door in the back.

"I can tell you're jazzed," he smiled, taking her hand. "Your eyes are shining like headlights."

"It was great. *You* were great. I don't know how you don't get killed riding those huge bulls."

"I've been lucky but you also have to have intense concentration. Besides, I have great motivation."

She tilted her head to look at him as they walked to his truck. "Oh?"

"I've been lucky all these years and I've got a nice stash of capital invested. My down payment on a ranch."

She didn't know what to say. Somehow she couldn't see him any place except on the circuit.

"Surprised?" His laugh had little humor in it. "Well, I guess I don't impress anyone as a ranch owner. But there's more to me than a fly-by-night good-time rodeo bum."

"Oh Ben." She squeezed his hand. It was warm against hers, the light contact sending tiny shivers racing through her body. "I didn't mean that at all. I was just surprised that you'd want to settle down, that's all."

"The life's beginning to wear on me, Grace. I want to quit before I'm crippled or dead." He opened the door and helped her up into the truck cab.

"Where do you think you'll go?" she asked when he climbed into the driver's seat.

"I've had my eye on a place up in Wyoming," he answered. "That's a real possibility."

Wyoming! I'll never see him again for sure. That's good though, right? This is just a…what? Time-out from my life?

"Now," he said, reaching over to caress her thigh. "That's enough of that for tonight. I just hope I can keep my hands to myself until we get to the hotel or we might have an accident."

Her heart was hammering with anticipation by the time Ben unlocked the door to his suite and flipped the light switch.

Grace caught her breath. Three large vases of roses overflowed on the round table by the window. On the credenza was a silver bucket filled with ice that held a bottle of champagne. Two flutes stood beside it. A note was stuck to the minifridge. "Everything is as you requested." Ben opened the door and gestured at the tray of strawberries and marshmallows dipped in chocolate chilling inside.

"My god, Ben, who were you expecting? Visiting royalty?"

He cupped her face with his hands. "You bet. Tonight you're my queen and you deserve royal treatment." His kiss was light and she felt the restraint he was forcing on himself. "Now. All day I've been imagining you tempting me with a striptease. Let's get some music, I'll pour some champagne and you can show me your moves."

"Oh." She stood stock still. "Striptease?"

"Yup. Come on. Don't disappoint me." He poured the golden liquid from the bottle into the flutes, handed her one and tapped hers with his. "To us. And a wonderful night of discovery."

Then he took her hand and led her into the bedroom.

While she sipped at the champagne, gathering her scattered courage, Ben turned on the stereo in the room, kicked off his boots and lay back on the bed.

"All right, darlin'. I'm ready."

Grace took a larger swallow of champagne, set the glass down and ditched her boots. Butterflies were doing their own dance in her stomach but when she saw the bulge behind Ben's fly and the heat in his eyes, her anxiety vanished and the remnants of last night's arousal flared to life.

She closed her eyes, took a deep breath and tried to remember every striptease movie or video she'd ever seen.

Letting the soft rhythm of the music flow through her, she began to move her hips in a slow bump and grind, dancing in place next to the bed. She opened each button on her blouse with slow deliberation, flicking the fabric each time it separated a little more. Her fingers brushed the pin and she took a moment to remove it and set it on the nightstand next to yet another vase of roses.

The heat in Ben's eyes flared as he watched her unbutton her cuffs and shrug the blouse off one shoulder at a time, finally letting it drop to the floor. Next came the button and snap on her slacks and she rolled them down her legs with tantalizing slowness. Having no idea where the courage or impetus came from, she stepped out of the slacks and stood with her feet apart, clad only in the thong and bra, tossing her head back and running her fingers through her hair.

"Jesus," Ben breathed, his hand cupping his crotch. "You are a walking wet dream."

A burst of excitement shot straight from Grace's brain to her cunt and she knew when she took off the thong it would be dripping with her juices. She did a quick bump and grind, thrusting her hips from side to side, tossing her head in time.

All those stripper movies at least taught me something.

"Shake those beautiful breasts for me," Ben encouraged.

Tossing down another swallow of champagne, Grace bent forward with her hands on her knees and shook her shoulders so her breasts swayed in time to the music.

Who am I? Where is this person coming from?

Ben rolled onto his side, reached out a hand and ran his fingers across the slope of her breasts. Her nipples hardened at once, poking against the sheer lace of the bra.

"I love the lingerie, darlin'," he told her in a warm, thick voice, "but I think it's time to take it off."

Fingers trembling, Grace opened the front clasp of the bra, pulled it away from her breasts and tossed it on top of her blouse. When she managed to wiggle out of her thong, she was embarrassed at how soaked it actually was. She would have thrown it on top of the growing pile but Ben's arm shot out and his hand gripped her wrists.

"I think that belongs to me." He plucked it from her fingers, crumpled it in his hand and held it to his nose, inhaling deeply. "The roses are no competition for this. Your scent is making me so hard I don't know if I can control myself." He switched the scrap of cloth to his other hand and pulled her forward, tumbling her to the bed.

Grace's heart was hammering in her ribs and her blood was pounding in her ears. She had an instinctive feeling that she was about to cross forbidden thresholds with this man and she wasn't sure she had the courage to do so. But then Ben leaned over her and took her mouth in a soul-devouring kiss and she forgot to think, forgot to be afraid, forgot about anything except the flame of his tongue in her mouth and his calloused hand cupping her breasts.

She moaned against his lips, shifting her hips, rubbing her bare skin against the rough weave of the fabric of his slacks. She wanted his hands on her as they'd been the night before, probing inside her, driving her to unexpected heights of pleasure.

"Will you do something for me?" he asked when he broke the kiss.

"Yes. I think. Maybe. What?"

"Spread your legs and touch yourself for me. Like you did last night, remember? You do that when you're alone, don't you?"

Grace didn't think it was possible for her face to get any hotter but she was sure someone had touched a match to it. How could she let him see her do something she did beneath her bed covers, not even exposed in the privacy of her bedroom?

"Gracie?" His tongue tickled her ear and his fingers tugged at one nipple, teasing it to fullness and brushing the rough surface of his fingertip across away it. "Can you do that for me?"

"Ben, I don't think… I mean…I've never…"

"Okay. I have an idea."

Desiree Holt

She frowned when he rolled off the bed, wondering what he was going to do next. He opened and closed a dresser drawer, then lay down beside her again, one of his bandanas in his hand.

Grace wet her lips with the tip of her tongue. It was strange enough that she was lying here stark naked while Ben was still fully clothed. *Now* what did he have in mind?

Is he into kinky stuff? Like I'm reading about? Am I?

"What's that for? What are you planning to do with it?"

He grinned. "Nothing exotic. At least," he added in a low voice, "not yet. I thought if I blindfold you, that way you can pretend you're in the room all alone and you won't be as self-conscious about this." He nipped the spot on her neck that she'd discovered was a highly sensitive erotic zone. "Come on, darlin'. Let's experiment a little, okay? I promise it will be worth it."

"Are you going to take your clothes off?"

Heat danced in his eyes and the whiskey color deepened almost to black. "Without a doubt. But not until after."

"After what?"

His voice dropped even lower. "After I watch you get yourself off. That is one of the sexiest things a man can see. A total turn-on. So are we good to go here?"

"A-All right." *Why not? Aren't I in this for the adventure? To test myself?*

She closed her eyes and lay stiffly while he placed the folded fabric across her eyes and tied it behind her head.

"Relax, darlin'. Pretend it's a game. One you're playing by yourself." He brushed his hand across her nest of pubic curls. "Such soft hair on this pretty little cunt. I'd love to see it bare." He ruffled the curls again, then ran his fingers through them. "Grace?"

"Mmm?"

"Did you ever think of shaving it?"

62

She had but she was again too embarrassed to tell him that. After one of the movies she'd watched, she stood in front of her full-length mirror for a long time, contemplating doing the task, then shoved it back onto her mental maybe-to-do list.

"Too shy to answer?" He chuckled as if he sensed her thoughts. "Good. Gives me a goal to work toward. Tell you what. You let me watch you play with yourself and I'll be your personal barber. Come on, darlin'. You can't imagine how hot it will make me. And I'll return the favor."

Grace finally nodded. She drew in a deep breath, held it, let it out and let her hands drift down between her legs. Automatically her thighs widened to give her better access.

"That's it. That's what I want to see. Slide your fingers down into your pussy and show me how wet you are."

Hidden behind the darkness of the blindfold, she stroked her hand through her folds, then lifted her fingers for Ben to see. His tongue swept across the tips, making her shiver.

"Your cunt is so juicy. Bend your knees and slide two fingers into it. Let me see you probe yourself."

Her fingers slid in easily and she moved them in and out two or three times.

"Feel good?" Ben asked. "I'll bet it does."

Grace thought about all the times she'd secretly finger-fucked herself before she'd bought her new toys and her hand moved in remembered motion. Up and down the length of her slit, one fingertip rimming the opening of her vagina, feeling the flesh warm to her touch and the special pulse begin beating deep inside her womb.

Ben moved again beside her, his arm brushing her tummy as he reached across her, then she felt the soft petals of a rose dancing across her flesh in cadence with her hand.

"That's it, darlin'. Keep right on fucking yourself while these roses kiss your skin. Do you like the feel of them?"

It really is like a kiss, Grace thought, like velvet lips whispering over her nerves, caressing her. The more Ben stroked them back and forth, the more aroused she became.

"I had high hopes for this, you know." His voice was like erotic music in her ear. "I bought some scented shaving gel today. Hoping, you know? Smells real sweet, just like your little puss. After I watch you bring yourself off, I'm going to cover that sexy little mound with that stuff, work it up into a lather, then carefully shave off every strand of hair, all the way down to your cute little asshole."

Grace's hand stilled for a moment as his words penetrated.

"Yes, darlin'. Right down to your asshole. Not a hair in sight anywhere."

Grace's hand moved faster up and down her slit, while the fingers of her other hand stole to her clit and began rubbing it. The pulse deep inside her throbbed with greater insistency as she visualized what Ben was describing.

"Then, when it's as slick as glass, I'm going to kneel between these lush thighs of yours that I thought about all day. I'll pull them over my shoulders so your cunt is wide open to me and plunge my tongue inside. I'm going to eat you as if you're my last meal ever, drinking up your juices, nibbling on your gorgeous clit. I'm going to use the tip of my tongue on that little nub until you scream for relief."

Faster, she told herself, her cunt pulsing as if she could almost feel his mouth on it. She pulled and tugged at her clit as she did in her bedroom, pinching it between her fingertips.

"Inside, Grace." His voice was rough with desire. "Shove your fingers inside and I'll give you something to think about."

She slid two fingers inside her pussy and began to fuck herself as she worked her clit harder and harder. Her breathing was ragged and she could feel her blood racing through her veins.

His hand moved to her other breasts, his finger flicking at the nipple, then rolling it between thumb and forefinger.

"I don't want to scare you off, Gracie, but I want to do so many things with you. Everything." The rose swished back and forth. "Even things you've never dreamed about. Do you have erotic dreams, where you do wild, wicked things?"

God, do I.

"Are you getting close?" he asked, trailing the rose down the inside of one thigh.

Now! She was shouting it in her head. *Now, now, now.*

Grace hitched her hips, riding her fingers, rubbing her clit. She was so close. So close. When she reached the moment where she usually squeezed her legs together, using her thighs like a vise on her hand, Ben moved and placed his hands on her thighs, spreading them as wide as he could.

"No," she cried. "I need…I need…

"*I* need to see that little cunt pulse and throb for me." He moved her hand out of the way and tugged the lips of her pussy until it was completely open. "Pinch your clit real hard, Gracie. Now. Right now."

She couldn't stop, couldn't not do it. She raked her fingernail over her clit and pinched it as hard as she could. Her orgasm exploded, her body arched and she felt her vagina spasm over and over again. The tip of Ben's finger traced the opening and slid inside, not nearly enough to fill her, just enough to tease her more and prolong the spasms.

"Jesus." Ben's breath hissed through his teeth. "That is one gorgeous, mouthwatering sight. You should see how it grips my finger, sucking it inside. That's what those tight, sweet muscles do to my cock, Gracie. God, just the thought of it almost makes me come like a horny teenager."

"Please," she begged, reaching to slide her fingers inside herself.

But Ben moved her hand out of the way and shoved three fingers inside her, twisting his wrist to create the friction she needed.

She pressed herself down on them as the spasms grabbed her, washing over her, rising up from deep in her womb and spreading throughout her body. Ben curved his fingers until the tips hit her sweet spot and the convulsions rocked her even harder, pushing her to the next level of pleasure.

"Scrape your clit," he whispered in her ear. "Keep doing it. Don't stop."

She dragged her nail back and forth over the sensitized nub, screaming with the pleasure-pain of it, her hips bucking like a wild horse as every pulse in her body shook her.

He was good, working her just right to bring her down slowly, his fingers massaging her vaginal walls as the quivers died down, her cream flooding his hand and running in a stream down between the cheeks of her ass to that tight sphincter. Finally, exhausted, she let her hands fall to her sides and her head drop back on the pillows.

Ben slipped off the blindfold, pushed the damp hair from her forehead and feathered kisses over her face. "Thank you for that, darlin'. It was...incredible. Totally incredible." He lifted one of her hands and placed it over his crotch. "Feel that? That's why my clothes are still on. Because the minute I let my cock loose I'll hardly have any control left. And I want this to last. A long time."

Grace turned her face and smiled at him. "Me too. But I think I need to catch my breath." She lowered her eyelashes. "You know, I'm not a big talker where sex is concerned but I never had an orgasm like that when I was alone."

"Good." He kissed the tip of her nose. "I want to keep it that way. Come. Sit up. Time for some champagne, then the barber will go to work."

Chapter Six

ଛୀ

The champagne was still chilled and the cool liquid felt good sliding down her throat. How was it possible, Grace wondered in amazement, to give herself an orgasm that was so powerful? She picked up the rose that Ben had left lying on her thigh and brushed the petals against her cheek. Her cowboy had a romantic streak. Who'd have thought it, from his hard, rough edges?

She heard him in the bathroom, moving around. When he came back into the bedroom he was carrying a small tote bag and a bowl of water, a large bath towel and a washcloth draped over one arm. He'd removed his shirt and once again she was breathless at the sight of his hard, muscular chest and the thick pelt of black hair covering it.

He took the champagne flute from her hand, finished the amber liquid in the bottom of it and set it on the nightstand. He set the bowl down next to it and Grace could see it was filled with water.

"Let's get comfortable, shall we, darlin'?"

Her breath hitched a little as she eyed everything in his hands, realizing she was about to cross into yet another area of sexual play and activity that up until now she'd only read about. Not that she hadn't imagined someone doing it to her. And now it was going to happen. Besides, Ben's smile was so sinfully seductive at that moment she would have done anything for him. With him.

"Tell me what to do."

Ben knelt on the floor in front of her, turning her sideways so her hips were on the edge of the bed He placed one pillow under her head and another, covered with the big towel, beneath her hips. Balancing the bowl on the bed next to her, he draped her legs over his thighs.

"Ready?"

"Yes." Then she caught the look on his face, as if he could devour her with one bite and she felt more feminine than she had in years. "Absolutely."

He soaked the washcloth in the warm water and wet her curls until they were well and truly soaked. Reaching into the little tote bag, he pulled out a long plastic tube, uncapped it and squeezed the scented gel into his hand. The aroma of crushed roses drifted into the air.

"Carrying out the theme?" she asked, as if talking would help her maintain a semblance of calm.

"I aim to please," he told her. "Like it?"

"Yes. Roses are my favorite."

"Well, see there? I lucked out on the first try."

He rubbed the gel into the curls on her mound, working it into a rich lather, then squeezed out more and massaged it into her labia and down to her ass. Just the touch of his fingers was making her hot again and she was sure cream was gathering in her cunt once more. When Ben circled her vaginal opening with his fingertip and smiled, she knew she was right. Heat crawled up her entire body.

Ben laughed. "I don't think I've ever seen anyone blush all over before."

Grace lifted her hands and moved to cross them over her chest but Ben shook his head.

"Don't. I like it. It matches the flowers. Okay, here we go."

The razor, pink to complement the roses—and wouldn't she have given anything to see him buying it—glided with smooth strokes across her mound. After each pass Ben swirled it in the water to clear it and went back to work.

The process was almost hypnotic. Glide, swirl, swish, then repeated all over again. When he nudged her thighs she let her knees fall open to give him greater access. With very gentle fingers he took her labia between thumb and forefinger and very, very carefully stroked the razor over the curls there.

She forced herself not to twitch as he reached the more sensitive areas. He soothed her by kissing the insides of her knees and blowing across the newly naked skin and making soft murmuring sounds to her.

"Almost done," he said, swishing the razor again. "I'm going to bend your legs way back toward your chest, so pretend you're a circus acrobat, okay, Gracie?"

It actually made her laugh and took the edge off her nervousness.

"Go ahead. My Pilates keeps me limber."

"Grab onto your knees so you don't lose your balance," he told her, placing her hands where he wanted them.

"Tell me this is sexy, okay?"

He trailed his finger the length of her slit. "You have no idea how sexy this is."

When he had her positioned the way he wanted her, he spread a generous amount of the gel on the entire area around her anus. He held her firmly so she wouldn't jump at the first touch of the razor in that sensitive area. He worked swiftly, knowing she was still edgy about him shaving her there.

At last he was finished, wiping away the last traces of the gel with the warm cloth, and set everything aside.

"I only took a quick shower after the events tonight," he told her, "and I want to make sure we get that sweet little puss clean so I can eat my fill."

As he helped her off the bed, Grace shivered just thinking of his tongue lapping at her, probing her, his mouth sucking on her tender flesh like he had the night before.

In what seemed like seconds Ben had disposed of the shaving equipment and stripped off the rest of his clothes. Sweeping her up in his arms, he carried her into the bathroom and turned on the shower.

"Just don't move," he told her, setting her on her feet and spreading her legs wide. "Stay right there."

With the water misting around them, he knelt before her, opened the lips of her pussy and began to lick her with slow strokes of his tongue. Her knees wobbled and Grace clutched at his shoulders to support herself, knowing in the back of her mind that she was losing her balance in more ways than one. And would probably never get it back.

* * * * *

Bringing Grace to climax in the shower had nearly finished Ben off. He wanted this to last, to take forever but he was so hard, so ready it took every ounce of his self-control. He let his fingers idly trace a pattern on the soft skin of the woman next to him. He loved the feel of her body. Her soft breasts with their rosy nipples and darker areolas surrounding them. He could see the pounding of her pulse in the hollow of her throat, the place he loved to tease with the tip of his tongue.

"Your body is incredible," he told her, anger rising when she turned away as if she didn't believe him.

"It's definitely on the downhill slide," she told him, punctuating her words with a deprecating laugh.

"Damn it, Grace," he swore. "I've been around the block more times than a taxi and I *know* what's good and what's not. So quit doing this to yourself and let me enjoy being with you."

He'd have to figure out a way to break her of the habit of downplaying herself. Didn't she have any idea how tempting she was? When he'd eaten her out in the shower he'd had to use every bit of control to keep from climaxing and embarrassing himself. God, she was so sweet and juicy and fresh as a newly picked peach. When he carried her back to the bed he'd taken all the roses from the vase on the night table and scattered the petals over her, crushing their fragrance into her skin.

He reached for the baby powder he'd had sense enough to buy today, carefully soothed the newly shaved skin of her cunt, then finally, finally, pulled on a condom and allowed himself to sink into her. But now that he was filling her tight, hot channel, now that her muscles were clasping at him like a rigid fist, now that he could feel his pubic hair rubbing against her naked mound, he had to force himself not to move. Now he wanted to stay where he was, reveling in the sheer lust that consumed him.

Tonight had been a test. Not for Grace but for himself. To see if what he felt last night was an aberration or if he still got harder than a railroad spike the minute he saw her. If he wanted to sink into her body forever. Well, he'd certainly found out and he had no idea what the hell to do about it.

In another week he'd be gone. Grace certainly wasn't a woman to traipse after a man on the circuit, nor did he want to put her out there for others to try for. Maybe if he didn't feel so used up he could try to look past the end of this event but he'd lived too hard and too fast for someone like Grace. He was damn lucky to have this time with someone like her at all.

Helping her discover her sexuality was an incredible turn-on. She was such a curious mixture of shyness and eagerness, of wariness and curiosity. But each time he got past one of her fences, she exploded like dynamite. The sight of her naked cunt was one he'd carry with him forever. If he could just hold onto her until the rodeo moved on, coax her into trying more things, open herself up more to him, at least he'd have memories to wrap around himself when he hit the road. And hopefully, he'd leave Grace with some hot ones of her own.

He rolled his hips a tiny bit, feeling her inner muscles grip him harder and he bent his head to capture one of her plump nipples in his mouth. He loved the taste and feel of it, soft yet hard at the same time, the pebbled surface slightly rough against his tongue. He pressed it against the roof of his mouth, rubbing it back and forth before taking a long pull at it. The simple sensations sent pleasure spiking through him and he dug deep to hang onto his control.

She was rocking her hips against him now, her cunt pulling at him. Even through the thin latex of the condom he could feel the flexing of every muscle, the liquid heat surrounding his cock. He couldn't remember the last time a woman turned him on this much. After she'd left this morning he'd gone back to bed but instead of sleeping he'd let images of her travel through his mind. Along with visions of every erotic thing he wanted to do to her.

Slow. He'd have to take it slow. Get her to commit one day at a time. And already he knew what he was planning for tomorrow night.

Her soft hands moved up to grip his shoulders and she wound her legs around his waist, locking him against her.

"Now, Ben." Her voice was heavy with desire, her eyes clouded with it. "I want you now."

Damn good thing too, because he couldn't hang onto it any longer. Streaks of lightning shot up his spine, his balls tightened and with a roar he thrust one final time and exploded inside her. She convulsed with him, shivering and shaking, chanting his name, meeting him thrust for thrust. The harder he pushed, the more she pushed back, digging her heels into the small of his back as if she'd never allow them to be separated.

Wet flesh met wet flesh and ragged breaths cut the still air in the room.

Soon the shudders became shivers and the shivers became twitches and then their bodies were still, glued together. His blood roared in his ears as his heart threatened to pound out of his chest.

* * * * *

Each time Grace thought she'd reached the absolute pinnacle of sensation, Ben found a way to drive her higher. All her "safety locks", the things that had kept her together for twenty years, seemed to be opening and letting loose a woman she didn't even know. As she lay exhausted in his arms, she wondered how soon the balloon would drop. When he would decide he'd had enough of being a teacher and wanted a woman more experienced. More…knowledgeable. More…something.

She felt his body shift and one hand lifted to brush the damp strands of hair from her face.

"I think it's time for some rules," he told her, his voice still raspy.

"Rules?" She frowned. "What kind of rules?"

"The rodeo isn't over for another week, Grace. I want to see more of you while I'm here." He rubbed his neck. "I don't think either of us is looking for anything beyond that, right?"

He could tell from the startled look in her eyes she hadn't even thought of that. Good.

"We can get to the how and when later," he went on, "but for however long we do this, Rule Number One is you do *not* say one negative thing about yourself. You're such a smart, beautiful, sexy woman." He brushed a kiss across her lips. "Say it, Gracie. Repeat those words."

"But—"

"Repeat them," he insisted.

She bit her lip, then forced out the words. "I am a smart, beautiful, sexy woman."

"See?" He licked the column of her throat. "That wasn't so hard, was it?"

"No." She couldn't help the sigh that escaped her. "At least, not *too* hard."

"Rule Two," he continued. "We are going to enjoy each other. Every way possible. You have such untapped sexuality, Grace. It would be a shame not to explore it."

"E-Every way possible?" Her voice was unsteady, her eyes searching his.

He nodded. "Whatever we *both* enjoy. But I want you to let me introduce you to pleasures you haven't even dreamed of. I've never wanted to do this with a woman before. To teach you what you've been missing."

"And if I say it's too much?"

"Then we won't go there. But Rule Three is, you're going to at least give me a chance."

She nibbled on her lower lip, swamped by conflicting feelings of erotic arousal and fear of the unknown. She could hardly believe she'd been so uninhibited with Ben these past two nights. Okay, so he wasn't tired of being the instructor yet. But she wondered just how much farther she could let him push her. Or if she could handle many more nights with him, even as her body craved it. And what would happen if she wanted to stop.

"How about it, darlin'?" His hand caressed the column of her neck, his fingers trailing down to brush across her nipples. "Sound okay to you?"

She blew out a long breath. "How about… Can we take it one night at a time? And see where it goes? I mean, when the rodeo leaves, you'll be gone too, right?"

He nodded. "I made no secret of that." He studied her face. "But I don't get the impression you're looking for anything beyond that either."

She gave a breathy little laugh. "I was hardly even looking for this. So…one night at a time, okay?"

"If that's what you want."

His hand was making tiny circles on her tummy, sliding ever closer to her mound. A fluttering of muscles in her cunt told her just how easily he could drive her up that erotic roller coaster.

"I've never..."She stopped and bit her lip. She seemed to be saying that a lot.

"Done anything like this?" he finished for her. "Grace, don't you think I know that? That's what's so delicious. I get to be your first for so many things."

"What kind of things?"

He saw the pulse at the hollow of her throat beat erratically.

"One of these nights, Gracie darlin', when you're ready, I'm going to fuck that gorgeous asshole of yours."

She jerked at his words and he saw a mixture of trepidation and anticipation chase itself across her face. "My...my..."

He grinned at her reluctance to even use the word.

"Shake you up a little? We'll take it real, real slow. But trust me, Grace. That ass will be mine." He bit her neck gently again. "Do you have a vibrator, Grace? I'll bet you do. Bring it with you tomorrow night. You know what I imagined this afternoon? Handcuffing you to this bed and teasing you with a vibrator until you screamed with pleasure."

She rolled toward him and in her eyes he could see every conflicting emotion. And beyond that a blaze of heat. Oh yes. It might not be tomorrow night but she would do these things with him. *For* him. But she took so long to answer he was afraid he'd read her wrong.

"Okay." She blurted out the word, her gaze sliding away from his.

"Okay?" he cupped her chin and forced her to look at him. "Rules and all?"

She nodded. "Rules and all."

75

He lifted his hand and threaded his fingers through her tousled hair. "Let's seal it with a kiss. And a lot more."

As they fell asleep he realized they never did get to the strawberries and marshmallows.

Chapter Seven

❧

Grace was thankful for the amount of work waiting for her on her desk. It meant she could focus her brain on numbers, not on the pleasurable aches in her body, or the limited amount of asleep she'd had. Ben had driven her home at six thirty, kissed her senseless before letting her out of the car and driven off with a reminder he'd be looking for her at the same spot tonight.

They'd had one minor disagreement—okay, argument— on the way to her house. He'd tried his best to convince her to move into the hotel with him for the rest of the rodeo but the thought made her uneasy. She knew herself, knew she needed an escape, a way out if it all became too much for her. Everything was happening so fast she couldn't keep up with it. And she still wasn't sure she was capable of seeing him again. He made her feel different. Vulnerable. Things she couldn't even explain.

She'd raced from the truck when he pulled into her driveway, waving goodbye as she shoved open her front door and fell inside. She'd done it again. Given herself to this man in ways more intense and erotic than she could ever have imagined. And the degree of pleasure she received from it actually frightened her. She wanted to wrap her safe life around herself and hide from her new and intense feelings.

Absently she rubbed the boot pin on her collar. She knew it was her imagination but the little piece of jewelry seemed hot to her touch, almost vibrant. The words of the woman who'd sold it to her kept drifting into her mind, *This pin will unlock those doors you hide behind.*

Grace dropped her hand as if it truly was on fire. What foolish nonsense, to think a pin could have any kind of influence on a person's life. And how idiotic of her to even pay attention to the woman's stupid prattling. She'd been taken with the pin despite her protests, so she'd let Melanie splurge on it for her. That was all.

Of course, she mused, it did bring her together with her lover but would she have met Ben anyway? Let herself experience two totally hedonistic nights?

Heat surged through her body as she remembered everything they'd done during the past two nights. She wiped her suddenly sweating palms on her skirt and tried to quell the mixture of desire and anxiety bubbling inside her. Too much, she told herself. She wasn't used to all this intense sexual activity and she suddenly felt overwhelmed by it all.

She'd agreed to see Ben again tonight but panic was wrestling with desire. She needed to back off a little. She'd leave him a message when she knew he'd be out of the room. It would make him mad but she couldn't let him persuade her to change her mind.

The buzzing of the office intercom pierced her mental battle with herself. She depressed the button.

"Yes, Joyce."

"Mr. Sanderson is on line two. He asked to speak with you. Are you in or out?"

Curt Sanderson. Delivered as if in answer to a silent prayer. Fifty-nine years old, he'd come to her as a client two years ago, recommended by a mutual friend. Since then he'd tried every way possible to get her to date him and so far she'd been able to gracefully refuse. He was settled, stable and wealthy. And like the few other men she'd permitted in her life, bland, smooth and colorless. And boring.

But maybe boring was what she needed right now. It was a lot safer than the red zone she'd fallen into. And Curt, fifteen years older than she was, would certainly never demand that she open her body to him in the ways that Ben did.

He was the first client she'd dated. Their first dinner together she'd pigeon-holed as a business discussion. And a need to get out of the office and breathe air in a different environment. She'd continued to see him very occasionally because he was exactly what he appeared to be and nothing more. Safe. Non-threatening. A man she could write off with one excuse or another and do it politely enough he wouldn't be offended. Like she did with the others. *Safe* required nothing of her.

Ben Lowell was certainly far from safe. He made her blood boil and her juices flow, found that hidden flame of desire she didn't even know she had and fanned it into a raging inferno.

Curt would be a good neutralizer for her out-of-control libido.

"Put him on," she told Joyce.

"Grace, good morning." His voice slid through the connection.

"Good morning, Curt. Is there something I can do for you? I thought the quarterly reports were all in order."

"They were fine," he assured her. "As always. Your work is impeccable." He paused. "I thought I'd make my usual pitch and see if maybe this time I could persuade you to have dinner with me? It's been a long time since our last one. There's a terrific new Italian restaurant that's opened on the Riverwalk. I understand their food is great and they have an excellent wine cellar. How about it? Is this my lucky day?"

Why not? I need to step away from Ben before he swallows me whole.

Wondering if she'd regret it later, she said, "Why, Curt, I think that would be very nice."

"My god, did you actually say yes?"

Grace laughed. She could imagine the shocked look on his face. "I did. See? Persistence pays off."

"I'll pick you up at seven, if that's all right with you."

For a moment she was tempted to tell him she'd made a mistake but she swallowed her words. "Seven will be fine."

She sat with her hand on the receiver after she'd hung up, still trying to convince herself she'd done the right thing. On impulse she unpinned the little boot from her collar and dropped it into her purse. There. She might not be superstitious but it was better not to take chances. Clearing her throat, she dialed the number of Ben's hotel and asked to be connected to his room.

Please don't let him be there. Please, please, please.

She clutched the receiver so tightly her fingers hurt.

"I'm sorry but the room doesn't answer," the operator told her. "Would you like to leave a message? I can put you through to voice mail."

Relief whooshed through her. Yes. A message. She wouldn't have to confront him. She'd worry about his reaction another time.

"Yes, please." When the recorded tone beeped at her, she got it all out as quickly as she could. "Hi, Ben. Sorry to leave you a message like this but something came up and I won't be able to make it tonight." Then, "Bye," and she hung up before she could change her mind.

She leaned back in her chair, shaking. He'd be mad. No, furious. Outraged. He wouldn't take kindly to being brushed off like this. On the other hand, maybe he'd be glad to be rid of her and find someone else.

No, not Ben.

Sighing, she managed to push it all from her mind and turn back to the file open on her computer. One thing at a time, she told herself. Maybe Curt Sanderson had somehow morphed into a hot, sexy hunk who could get her juices flowing. If not, so much the better. Curt was *safe*. Settled.

Predictable. All the things that Ben was not. But all the things the sensible side of her brain told her she needed in her life, not some rodeo drifter taking her on a wild ride.

* * * * *

By seven thirty Grace knew her idea had been foolish if not downright idiotic. Almost from the moment Curt had ushered her into the restaurant and they'd followed the maitre d' to their table, she knew this was a mistake.

As she sipped her wine from the oversized goblet, she let her eyes roam over every detail of the man across from her that she could see, hoping she was missing something. But no, it was the same old Curt. The one who had seemed like such a good candidate for socializing. A carbon copy of the other men she'd allowed herself to date since she took down the Keep Away sign. Gray hair combed so carefully not one strand would dare move out of place. Closely shaven face pink from the effects, she was sure, of the three glasses of wine he'd already had to her one. Suit almost the same shade of gray as his hair. With his impeccably laundered white shirt and precisely knotted tie, he looked like a cover model for a senior citizen's magazine.

But Curt no longer appeared to her as a person who was aging gracefully as she'd once thought. Already she could see the hint of jowls along his jawline and the beginning of liver spots on the backs of his hands. He never worked out, didn't even play golf and she wondered now if the body beneath the expensive tailoring was already showing the first signs of flab.

Thinking of him naked, a shiver of revulsion raced over her that she could barely control.

What am I thinking here? Curt is exactly what I need. The perfect…the perfect…the perfect what?

The perfect waste of time, her mind screamed at her. Put him next to Ben and there was no comparison.

Ben!

Get out of my mind. I need to stop thinking about you.

"Grace?"

She jerked herself back to the present, realizing Curt was talking to her.

"I'm sorry," she apologized. "Just winding down from the day. What were you saying?"

He reached across the table and closed his hand over the one she had resting on the fine linen. It took all her willpower not to jerk it away.

"I was just remarking how nice it is to finally spend some time with you again that doesn't involve my business."

"Oh. Yes. Thank you."

Her mind blanked and she sipped at her wine. Without thinking her hand stole to the pin she'd placed on the lapel. She had no idea what had made her fasten it on at the last moment. Now it was like a flame thrower burning a hole into her body. The tip of one finger rubbed the burnished surface and instantly an image of a naked Ben flashed across her brain.

No, no, no! This is what I'm trying to get away from.

Ben Lowell had *Danger — Handle With Care* written all over him. The intensity of what was building between them scared her to death, so she'd run back to what was safe. Secure. Nonthreatening. Curt Sanderson.

But when you danced with the devil, you couldn't slow down for a sedate waltz. All that wild music just keeps on playing, drawing me in. I'm afraid to lift the cover and look inside myself. So here I sit, time moving as if weighted by concrete.

She had no idea how she got through the rest of the dinner. Of course she had no one but herself to blame. She was careful never to leave her hand where Curt could grab it again, or to lean forward in an attitude he could in any way consider intimate. She forced herself to eat enough of her meal so he wouldn't question her lack of appetite but everything she chewed tasted like sawdust.

This was a stupid idea. Stupid, stupid, stupid.

And she'd broken one of her firm, cardinal rules. Don't date clients.

Thinking she could wipe away traces of Ben by having dinner with Curt was a big mistake. She might as well admit to herself she was hooked on the rodeo cowboy with a desire so intense it almost frightened her.

Letting Curt's prattle drift over her head, she tried to imagine him naked in bed. Wondered how inventive he'd be. How quickly he got hard and how long he could hold it.

Jesus! What's happening to me?

But the visions, rather than arousing her, made her nauseous.

Now she sat here with a pounding headache trying to keep a polite smile on her face and not to sneak a look at her watch. Finally she gave up the ghost.

"Curt, I'm so sorry." She leaned forward, rubbing her temples with her fingertips. "I just can't seem to get rid of this headache. Would you mind very much taking me home?"

He pressed his lips together then forced a smile. "Of course. I hope it isn't the company."

"Not at all." *Liar!* "I've enjoyed myself tremendously." *You'll go to hell for that one.* "Maybe we could do this again sometime." *Like in another life.*

"You work too hard," he told her, signaling for the check. "I tell you that all the time. You should hand off more to the people who work for you."

"You know I'd never have anyone else handle my special clients like you." *Maybe I should flutter my eyelashes too. How disgusting I am.* "And thank you for being so understanding."

"Not at all. As long as I get another shot. I've enjoyed myself tremendously." He scribbled his name on the charge slip, then rose and held her chair for her.

Grace tried to stay far enough ahead of him as they headed toward the restaurant door but Curt was right there beside her. His hand on her elbow made her skin crawl. As soon as they reached the front of the building and he gave his ticket to the valet she moved away, out of reach.

The drive home seemed almost as interminable as the dinner. Not just because she had to face the fact that Curt was an incredible bore and physically unappealing to her. No, it was more than that. She was running away from herself as a woman. From her needs. Her wants. Only the place she thought she could run to was suddenly no longer attractive to her.

The moment the car pulled into her driveway she had her door open and was heading toward her porch, keys in hand. When she turned to say good night, Curt was so close she could count the threads in his shirt. She forced her hand up between them and grabbed his, shaking it.

"Good night, Curt. Thank you very much. The dinner was terrific."

Liar.

He leaned forward slightly, his intent very clear but the last thing in the world she could stomach was a kiss from this man. She shoved her front door open and smiled over her shoulder.

"Thanks again, Curt. I'll be talking to you soon."

Inside she closed the door and leaned against it, waiting for the sound of the car leaving. Finally she pushed herself away and headed toward the kitchen for a glass of water, only to hear a loud knocking on the door.

Oh hell. Please don't let him be back here. I've had it for the night.

She wanted to ignore the summons but knowing Curt he'd stand there all night or call emergency services to see if she'd passed out. Pasting a smile on her face, she jerked the door open, ready with her excuses.

But it wasn't Curt standing on her porch. Instead an angry Ben Lowell pushed his way inside, slammed her door and bracketed her face with his hands before she could react. His mouth was inches from hers.

"Do you mind telling me," he asked in a voice taut with fury, "just exactly what the fuck that message was you left me and who the fuck you've just been out flouncing yourself around with?"

Grace's heart was beating so fast she was sure it would jump out of her chest and her mouth was suddenly so dry she couldn't form one word.

"Well?" His hot breath fanned her face and his eyes glittered like twin torches. "What's the matter? Cat got your tongue? Trying to think up an appropriate lie?"

"I-I-I was…out with a-a client," she finally stammered.

"A client." He spat the words out. "If that's what it really was, you could have asked me to call you and told me in person. I certainly understand that you run a business, Grace. But you leave me a message as if we've done nothing more than share a casual cup of coffee and had a *maybe* date you had to cancel. Shit, Grace. I thought we were well beyond that."

"I…I can't breathe," she gasped, needing to put some space between them.

At once he loosened the pressure of his hands and stepped back. "I'm sorry. I wouldn't hurt you for the world." A wicked grin tilted one corner of his mouth. "Except for pleasure, of course. You just made me so damn mad." His voice softened. "I missed you tonight, Gracie. And I was as jealous as hell when that guy pulled up in your driveway."

"He's just a client," she repeated, stepping back and taking a deep breath. "Nothing more." *And that's all he'll ever be, that's for sure.* "Nobody important."

"And what am I?" His voice was husky, with a slight catch in it. "Also nobody important?"

Grace had backed up into the living room, Ben following her, until the backs of her legs hit an armchair and she dropped into it gratefully.

"Well?" he persisted.

"You know better than that." She tried desperately to pull her scattered thoughts together.

"Then prove it. Let's go upstairs right now and make up for lost time."

Her breath caught in her throat. "Upstairs? In my room?"

That smile appeared again. "Unless you'd rather use one of the others."

Ohmigod. Have sex with Ben Lowell in my bedroom?

Somehow, keeping all this away from the house had made everything seem far enough removed that it didn't affect her regular life. Didn't actually seem real. More like acting out a scene from one of her books. But bringing him into her bed would personalize it. Break down the barriers she'd erected that allowed her the freedom to be someone else when she was with him.

"I...I can't do that, Ben." She gripped her hands together tightly in her lap, watching a hot flush creep up his cheeks.

"Why not?" The edge of anger was back, making his voice sound hard.

"I just can't." She twisted the folds of her skirt.

"Oh I see." He took a step back, angry understanding hardening his face. "I'm good enough to fuck in a hotel room but not here where you live. Where my scummy presence might invade your pristine life. Or dirty your pristine bed. Your life where you have everything organized so you won't have to *feel*. I'll bet you don't even color outside the lines, do you? Okay, okay. I get it. Your adventure to the underbelly is over. That's what your date with grandpa was about tonight, wasn't it?"

"No," she cried, "that's not it at all."

"It isn't?" He tilted his head. "Then what, Grace? What is it? Tell me, because I thought we had something good going here. Really great for the time it lasts."

She wet her lips. "I just… I think we need to take a step back. Take a breath. I feel as if I'm on a runaway train and the only way to stop it is to crash. Please understand," she begged. "This is all so new to me. So different. I just can't…"

"Can't what, Grace? Allow yourself to be human? To explore your sexuality? Or are you afraid you might enjoy things with me you never did with your husband and you'd be somehow disloyal? Is that it? Are you afraid to join the land of the living?"

Tears burned the back of her eyelids. "I don't know, Ben. I just know I need some space. Please."

He stood there, his fiery gaze raking her from head to toe and back. At last he took a step back.

"Fine. You can have all the space you want, Grace. But when you make up your mind, *you'll* have to come to *me*. And take a chance that I'll still be waiting."

He yanked the front door open then slammed it behind himself. Grace listened for the sound of his car pulling away before she allowed the tears to flow. Putting her head in her hands, she sobbed harder than she had since the day of Joe's funeral. She was just glad there was no one there to see it.

* * * * *

Ben floored the accelerator until he was out of sight of Grace's house, then turned a corner and pulled over to the curb, putting the gear shift in Park. The last thing he needed was a speeding ticket. For the first time since he'd gotten Grace's voice mail message he allowed himself to take a deep breath and ease the tension in his body.

He still didn't know why the hell he was so angry. Grace Delaney was just another woman, right? They'd had some outstanding sex but there were certainly a ton of other women out there who would eagerly share his bed. And his brand of sex.

Except he didn't want any of them. He wanted Grace.

And that bugged the shit out of him.

He was going against all his rules. All the *dos* and *don'ts* he'd set up years ago, to protect himself from choking entanglements. Everything that allowed him to control his life. Specific rodeos. Specific bulls he wanted to ride. Number of points he wanted to win each year. And mindless sex, so nothing endangered his plans for the distant future. He might look like a rodeo bum to Grace Delaney but he had plans and no one was going to interrupt them. Two or three more years at the most and he'd achieve his goal.

Because Ben Lowell had a secret. He rode the bulls for far more than the thrill of it. Entered the roping competitions for far more than showing off his skill. In all these years on the circuit he'd been stashing his winnings away. Hotshot always went first class, no scrimping there. And Ben always stayed in good hotels, his one concession to his beat-up body. But everything else went to help him reach his secret goal — buying a ranch.

Just as he'd told Grace, he wasn't stupid enough to think he could do this forever. At thirty-two he was already feeling his age and then some. He'd done some research, found someone he trusted and opened an investment account. Every time he got a check, a big chunk of it went to that pot of money, which, if his statements could be believed, was growing at a rapid rate.

He'd sworn to himself he'd never let some woman come along and get her hooks into it. When he left the circuit and settled down he'd take his time, choose just the right person. Someone who'd love the ranch life as much as he did and could see beyond his public image.

But Grace Delaney wasn't "some woman". She lit his fire in places he didn't know could be heated. In his dreams she tantalized and tormented him, her soft lips whispering to him as their bodies moved in an erotic dance. When he competed each night he found himself having to work hard to blot her out of his mind and concentrate on the competition.

All for a woman who was too fastidious to take him into her own bed in her own home. Make love with him in her own house. *Fuck him* in her own home, because that's what he wanted to do to her. His hotel room was fine but she had a big invisible fence around her life.

Well, that was what he'd wanted, right? No strings? Just sex?

What an ass he'd made of himself tonight, barging into her house that way. Demanding to know who she'd been with and what she'd been doing. Acting as if he owned her, for chrissake. Probably frightening the life out of her.

Good going, Ben. Way to seduce a woman.

So what? he answered himself. She *was* just "some woman" and he needed to get that straight in his mind. In frustration he banged his fist on the steering wheel. The hell with her. What did he expect anyway? Maybe that blonde who kept giving him the eye was still hanging around the hotel bar.

Taking the on ramp to the interstate, he gave the truck a little extra gas as he headed downtown.

* * * * *

Grace was exhausted by her tears, stunned by her reaction to what had just happened. She could still hear Ben's angry words vibrating in the air, see the rage mixed with hurt in his eyes.

You stupid old woman. What have you done?

Given in to her fears, that's what she'd done. Fallen right back into rigid Grace Delaney mode. Safe mode. Practically insulted a man who'd made her feel even more like a woman than Joe Delaney ever had.

And that was the problem.

She made herself move, picking up her purse she'd dropped on a chair, climbing the stairs to her bedroom on leaden feet. She flicked the switch that turned on the bedside lamp and stood in the doorway, studying the room.

Pristine, Ben had called it. Without ever even seeing it he was so right.

Thick white carpeting. Oyster white walls, unrelieved except for one pastel waterscape. Furniture such a pale shade of blue it almost looked white. She'd bought it when she found she could no longer sleep alone in the bed she and Joe had shared before his death. In the bed where they'd conceived two children in quick succession, children who never got to know their father, thanks to a drunk driver. A framed photo of those children—Bridget and Ryan—sat on the top of a dresser whose only other adornment was a gold-rimmed tray that held a brush and comb set at precise angles.

Even her wedding picture had been put away long ago, as she shut every vestige of emotion out of her life.

She'd done the same with everything else. Clung to the apartment as long as she could, then moved as soon as she could force herself to. First to the townhouse, then to this home. Investigated day care more intensively than the Secret Service. Kept a calendar on the refrigerator with everything neatly printed in squares.

Pristine barely began to describe the room. Or her life.

She realized with a shock that the reason she loved accounting so much was because everything was so neat and orderly. Little numbers went into little columns. Nothing messy. Nothing vital. Nothing she couldn't control.

Had she organized her life this way to eliminate the possibility of another catastrophe like the accident that took Joe's life? Did she think by controlling everything, nothing bad would ever happen again? If she didn't feel anything she couldn't possibly get hurt?

She wondered what her children, now in their early twenties, thought of her. How they saw her.

Her scared self had just thrown away the most enervating, soul-enriching thing that had ever happened to her. Sex with Ben wasn't dirty or seedy. He made her feel cherished, as if every act they performed together was an homage to her. Instead of embracing it fully, she'd run to a dull date with dull Curt and practically told Ben he wasn't good enough to be in her house.

What in hell was wrong with her?

Nothing. I made a stupid mistake that I won't repeat. That's what I get for reading erotic romances, daydreaming about posters and letting Melanie try to turn me into something I'm not.

Very carefully she undressed, hung her dress on a wooden hanger, took down her hair and brushed it thoroughly and washed the makeup from her face. Slipping into a nightgown, she folded back the covers, climbed into bed and sobbed until she had no more tears left.

Chapter Eight

ജ

Morning didn't make things look any better. Grace finally dragged herself to the office, hoping to bury herself in work. About midmorning Joyce came in carrying a very large florist box, grinning broadly.

"I wish you'd let me in on your tricks," she joked. "I think this is the biggest florist box I've ever seen. It's got to be from the guy with the hot voice."

Grace her breath caught in her throat. Was it possible? Was this his way of moving past the night before?

"I can't tell until I open it," she told her secretary.

Her fingers shook as she opened the book, separated the green tissue paper and pulled out the card. Hope fell in her like a rock in her stomach.

"Thank you for a lovely evening. I hope it's the first of many. Curt."

She shoved the box at Joyce. "Here. Find a vase for them and put them in the reception area where everyone can enjoy them."

Joyce frowned. "But—"

"Just do it," Grace snapped, then softened her voice. "Sorry. I'm just a little edgy this morning."

"Big night?" Joyce winked at her.

"Not exactly," she muttered, then waved her hand. "Go on. Let me get back to work."

She bent her head over the file on her desk, effectively shutting out further conversation.

"Those flowers can't be from Ben," she heard Melanie's voice say. "Not with the mood he was in last night."

Grace lifted her head and looked up.

Melanie tossed her purse on the couch and dropped onto the soft leather next to it. "So are you going to tell me what happened?" she demanded. "I thought you two were setting the city on fire."

"I don't want to discuss it." Grace looked away from her friend. "And what do you mean by 'the mood he was in'?"

Her friend shrugged. "He never hangs out at the usual bars the cowboys do after each night's events. He's kind of a loner. Doesn't run about with the buckle bunnies or pour down the booze. He's very, oh, I don't know, focused. That's it. Focused."

Grace knew she should just ignore the whole thing but she couldn't help herself. "So what does that have to do with last night?"

"He showed up at The Last Mile, a place near the arena everyone hangs out at, in the foulest mood I've ever seen anyone wear and proceeded to try to drink the bar dry." She snorted. "I think he was already well on the way when he got there because he mumbled something about the hotel bar."

Grace's eyebrows flew up to her hairline. "Ben? Are you talking about Ben Lowell?" In the short time they'd been together she was aware of that fact he measured his alcohol consumption very carefully.

"The very same. Care to tell me about it?"

Grace looked back down at the file folder again. "Not really. And I don't mean to be rude but I've got a lot of work piled up. This isn't a good time for me to visit."

"Visit?" Melanie was off the couch and in front of the desk in seconds. "Did you say visit? I'm not here on a social call. I want to find out what my *friend,* who I thought was finally letting herself live a little, did to screw things up."

"What *I* did?" Grace snapped the pencil in her hand as anger raced through her. "Why do you automatically assume I was the one who did something wrong? How do you know Ben Lowell isn't the culprit?"

Melanie leaned across the desk and cupped her hand under Grace's chin, forcing her to look up. "Because I know you, sweetie. And I bet I can put my finger on it. You decided you were having too good a time, right?"

"I don't—"

"Those new duds that show off a very sexy figure and a couple of nights tangling the sheets with a man I'd give my eyeteeth for scared the hell out of you, didn't they? Look at me, Grace. Don't shift your eyes away."

Grace threw the pieces of the pencil onto the desktop and tugged her head away from Melanie's grasp. "You're wrong. That's not it at all."

Liar!

"Then tell me what *did* happen. God knows Ross said he's never seen Ben in the state he was in last night. Any man in the world would have given a year's winnings to have all that naked flesh thrown at them."

Images flashed across Grace's brain of a very naked Ben on a king-sized bed with two or three or even four equally naked women doing things she probably hadn't even thought of yet. A sour taste filled her mouth and her stomach cramped. Well, it was her own damn fault. What did she expect? That he'd wait faithfully like some old dog for her to get over her jitters?

"I-I just asked him for some space," she protested. "That's all. What's wrong with that?"

Melanie huffed her impatience. "Space, huh? The man's in town for five more days. After that you'll have all the space you want. Did you stop to think of that?" She stared at Grace and the hard look on her face softened. "Don't worry. He didn't go off with anyone last night but it sure wasn't for lack of trying on anyone else's part. Ross and the chute master finally dragged him out of the bar and back to the hotel. I promise you he's got a hangover this morning the size of Texas."

Grace closed the folder on her desk and turned to her computer, effectively shutting Melanie out. She couldn't show any interest. She just couldn't allow herself.

"It's none of my business anyway. Thanks for coming by but I really have to get back to work."

There was a long silence then she heard Melanie moving to the couch, picking up her purse. "Suit yourself, kiddo. It's your funeral. And I do mean funeral. The death of what little fun you were allowing yourself. Me, I've got a lunch date I don't intend to miss."

"Have a good time," Grace muttered, banging away at the keyboard.

She heard the door open, then Melanie saying, "Give yourself a break, will you? Life is for the living, not the dead."

Then she was gone.

Grace leaned back in her chair, the headache she'd woken up with now pounding furiously behind her eyes. Again she thought of what Ben had said last night and her introspection about herself. She *hadn't* buried herself with Joe. She *hadn't*. But she wasn't living either and she'd just begun to realize it. And she'd probably killed the only chance to break free she'd had.

* * * * *

When Ben arrived at the arena he'd finally pulled himself together enough to ride tonight without killing himself. At least tonight's event for him was roping, not bull riding, and Hotshot would do most of the work. He just needed to make sure he concentrated.

Enough aspirin had reduced the pounding in his head from jackhammer strength to a dull throb. What a dumbass thing that had been, trying to drink the bar dry. He hadn't been that stupid in ten years. Of course he'd also been trying to forget what an ass he'd almost made of himself with the blonde bimbo in the bar, hoping he could erase the taste and scent of her with enough booze.

Why in the hell did he think he could blot out the impact of Grace Delaney, a true original, with a plastic blonde and her equally plastic boobs? If he'd had the courage he'd have taken an axe and chopped off his head. Or maybe his cock. Thank god he'd beaten it out of the bar before she could convince him to take her up to his room.

But that still didn't solve the problem of Grace. Too bad he'd let his stupid macho hormones blow it. He didn't own her. And he sure wasn't looking for a long-term relationship. He'd been very clear about that. But he thought they were both on the same page about enjoying each other while he was here. She'd agreed to The Rules, hadn't she? Grace was like a furled flower ready to open and taking her on a sexual journey was the most erotic thing he'd ever done.

He made his way into the huge dining hall, knowing he needed something light in his stomach before his event. The noise nearly took his head off, assaulting an already abused part of his body. He managed to get some coffee and a small bowl of stew and find himself a corner to hide in, careful to avoid Melanie and Ross. He needed to settle himself, get his event over with, then figure a way out of this mess.

Shit, shit, shit. He'd really screwed himself this time.

* * * * *

Grace leaned back in the tub, letting the bubbles tickle her chin and sipping the glass of chilled white wine. She hoped it would settle the very bad case of nerves that had her stomach jumping and her body trembling.

Well, isn't this a fine mess.

The last thing she'd expected when she let Melanie drag her to the rodeo and dump her into that large vat of testosterone was to meet someone like Ben and find herself in the middle of a sexual explosion. She couldn't avoid facing the fact that the intensity of her reaction to him, the things she responded to, had scared the hell out of her and sent her running back to the likes of Curt Sanderson.

She couldn't figure out if she was being sensible or a coward. She was only glad neither of her children lived at home to tune in to her mental chaos. They were better interrogators than the Grand Inquisitor. The problem was, she was sure she knew what they'd say. Both of them.

Bridget, in her first job with a public relations firm, reveling in the pleasure of living alone, would tell her to get out and live life. Enjoy herself. Don't let middle age take her over before it got there. Bridget herself was enjoying life sometimes to a point that Grace suffered anxiety attacks about it. Now she wondered if it wasn't a rebellion against the tight rein she'd kept on both kids all these years.

Ryan, although immersed in the fieldwork for his job as a geologist, would tell her not to fall for any phony baloney story and let some smooth talker get his hands on her money or her business. But then he'd tell her that at least once in her life she needed to take a chance. Just be careful.

Grace sighed. She'd left her office when her headache became unbearable, tired of trying to concentrate on work when all she could think about was Ben's hands and mouth on her, Ben's cock inside her. Time to pull her courage together and stop being a fraidy-cat. It was all right to like sex. Even to love it. And when would she ever have a chance like this again?

Of course, for all she knew, he'd found someone else to hook up with already. He'd been pretty angry last night, to a degree that really puzzled her. If this was just a here-and-now thing, why would he care if she saw someone else?

Stop it. You know why. He won't let you hide behind yourself and that's exactly what you were doing.

She finished the wine and let the water out of the tub. Drying herself on a fluffy towel, she rubbed fragrant cream onto every inch of her skin and into every crevice of her body. Sprayed a matching cologne at all her pulse points. On the way home she'd stopped at a boutique Melanie had once told her about and splurged on frothy pale peach lingerie, skintight jeans, a peach-colored shell and an embroidered blouse that she left open and knotted at the waist.

Brushing her hair until it fell in loose, shiny waves around her shoulders, she fastened gold studs in her ears, settled her western hat on top of her head. The last thing she did was pick up the little pin, glowing in the tray on her dresser, and pin it to the collar of her blouse.

All right, Grace. Here's where the rubber meets the road. Nothing ventured, nothing gained.

God, could she possibly think of any more clichés?

Picking up her purse, she gave herself one final look in the mirror and headed for the garage.

* * * * *

Ben took his time putting away his gear after his event. Somehow he'd found the grit and discipline to push everything from his mind the moment the chute door opened and he and Hotshot were after the calves. Another first place and hard won at that. The points were piling up. His last investment statement had shown a bigger growth than he'd expected. That meant he could move his plan forward. If he could just keep it together until the finals in Las Vegas, he'd finally have enough to buy that ranch, stock it and weather some lean years in the beef market. That's what was keeping him going.

But now he was facing the empty hours of the night, hours he'd hoped he'd be spending with Grace. Doing things that made his cock hard just thinking of them.

Maybe his mistake had been in pushing her so hard. In asking so much of her. In pushing her for a commitment to stay with him until the rodeo was over. She'd asked to take it one day at a time and he'd agreed, then tried to change things. She'd run back to her regular life, sending a message loud and clear.

After surviving the mother of all hangovers, getting through his event this evening — and winning, however the hell *that* had happened — and putting Hotshot away, he'd finally realized a fact that should have been staring him in the face.

Grace Delaney was flat-out scared. Not shy, not hesitant but totally freaked out. And not of him, not even of the things they'd been doing, but of herself. Of the sexuality she'd kept hidden all these years.

This was all uncharted waters for her. She needed the safety of her barriers. The separation of the different parts of her life. And she'd run back to whoever-the-hell the old goat was last night because he represented that safety to her.

Why hadn't he been able to see it?

Okay, so he was only here for a short time more. The clock was ticking. But somehow he'd turned it into a time bomb. Now it had blown up in his face. There was so much more he wanted to do with Grace, who now haunted his dreams. There was still so much of his lifestyle he wanted to introduce her to. She was like a flower unfolding and he wanted to peel back each petal.

Stupid thought but he'd had the feeling she'd been waiting just for him to come along. Now his temper had managed to screw it up.

Shit! Double shit!

Sighing, he said good night to everyone in the staging area and the guard at the back entrance and pushed open the back door.

And stopped, his jaw dropping.

He was sure he was imagining the vision leaning against the side of his truck, western hat tilted at a go-to-hell angle, lush body encased in the tightest jeans he'd ever seen. And on her face a very tentative smile.

All he could do was stand there and stare.

"You can tell me to go home if you want to," she said in a tremulous voice. "But the guard's going to think I'm a big liar because I told him you were expecting me. Besides, you'd have to find a cab since I left my car at home."

He knew he should move but he was frozen in place, his feet rooted to the spot.

"I guess that answers my question," she said, her voice tight, and pushed herself away from his truck.

That unglued his feet. Fast. He was on her in two seconds, his fingers grasping her upper arms, his eyes studying hers. He saw passion, hope, nerves — a potent emotional cocktail.

"I'm so sorry," he said, anxious to get that out right away.

"No." She shook her head. "I'm the one who's sorry. I was unbelievably rude to you."

He managed a small grin. "Not much else you could be to a man who storms into your home that way and rakes you over the coals." He let out a long, slow breath. "I'd like to go back to where we were before, Grace. Maybe even where we started. If that's possible."

"Not back," she said. She wet her lips with the tip of her tongue, a sure sign of her nervousness. "Forward. I want to go forward."

Forward. God, was it possible? Could he make this night the most memorable she'd ever spent? Push her beyond her limits without chasing her away? His groin tightened as images flew through his brain.

"Are you sure?" he asked. *Please let her be sure.*

She let out a slow breath. "Yes." Then, more firmly, "Yes, I am."

"Good. Me too. I want to keep going forward." He pulled out his keys and pressed the remote to unlock the truck. "Why don't we go to my hotel room and discuss it a little further."

Her lips trembled with a tiny smile. "Sounds like a plan to me."

* * * * *

She hadn't known what to expect when they got to Ben's suite. Maybe that he would rip her clothes off, throw her on the bed and ravish her. Tie her at once to the bedpost and attack her like someone on an overload of testosterone. Which no doubt he was, now that she thought about it. She probably could have handled that a lot better. It had less emotion wrapped in it. Just sex for the sake of sex.

But he'd apparently decided to take a different tack, determined to soothe her skittering feelings. To make her feel good. Relaxed. At ease, if that was possible.

She'd worn the little pin again, hoping it would bring her good luck, feeling its heat through the fabric of her blouse. It seemed to be more than doing its job. She wondered if she imagined the faint bloom of heat that spread from it throughout her body.

In the truck Ben called the hotel and asked them to send a cooler with wine, glasses and chocolate-covered strawberries up to his room and have them ready when he got there.

"We didn't get to them the last time," he chuckled. "Remember?"

She remembered all too well, heat dancing through her body like a devilish imp and sending more liquid to her panties.

Ben fiddled with the radio until he found a station playing soft mood music. Then he reached for her hand, lacing his fingers with hers.

"Ben, I don't—"

He lifted their joined hands to touch her lips.

"Hush," he told her. "It's all right. Just put your head back and enjoy the ride. You look wound up tighter than a rope on a charging bull."

He was certainly right about that. As much as she tried to calm herself, inside her butterflies were frantically beating their wings.

"Let me call the shots tonight, Grace. Let me take you to places you never thought you'd ever go."

Her heart raced and heat charged through her body.

The champagne and strawberries were waiting as promised when he opened the door to the suite. The first thing he did was toe off his boots and stand them to the side along with his Stetson. Then he nudged her into a chair, pulled her boots off and sat them next to his. He whistled softly as he poured their wine then turned on the stereo. She hadn't really notice before how cleverly it was concealed in an armoire.

Touching the rim of his glass to Grace's, he said "To a night of unbelievable pleasure."

"Unbelievable pleasure," she echoed nervously, nearly gulping her wine and wondering what was going on here.

Ben took the goblet from her and set both glasses on the table. As the music flooded the room, he pulled her into his body, both arms holding her against him as he moved them slowly to the rhythm of the song. His arms were strong around her, his big capable hands massaging the tense muscles in her back.

"Relax." His breath tickled her ear. "We may be going forward but we're going to take it slowly. Enjoy every step of the journey. Catch up on some things we missed the first time around. When was the last time you danced with anyone?"

Too long ago to remember.

"That long, huh?"

She didn't realize she'd voiced her thought out loud. "Dancing just hasn't been a part of my life for a long time."

"I think too many things haven't been a part of your life," he murmured. "Maybe ever. I blame myself for the way this played out. We sort of jumped into it with both feet. I was so hot for you the minute I saw you, I'm surprised I didn't lay you down on the seat of my truck and fuck you right then and there. Holding onto myself until we got to the hotel was an exercise in discipline for me."

His voice was like warm syrup, its deep tone sliding over her.

"Really?" *Well, Grace, could you sound any more idiotic?*

"You have no idea how aroused I was the first time I laid eyes on you. I thought I deserved a medal for what little restraint I had." He nibbled her earlobe. "But tonight you're going to get the full treatment, Gracie mine. You deserve it. Tonight we'll even get to the strawberries."

She wanted to protest that it was okay, she understood, except she felt so good she couldn't object to anything. For years she'd avoided any social interaction with men except for business and when she finally started dating, the men were all of an age where seduction was a long ago memory.

This...this was...nice. She let herself be molded to his body as they moved in slow rhythm to the music. His thighs pressed against hers and the thick ridge of his cock was evident even through their layers of clothing, as he moved them in a dance of miniscule steps. The heat of his body and the friction as his legs rubbed against hers made liquid drip from her cunt and soak her panties. She wondered if he could smell the scent of her sex through her slacks.

The tip of his tongue traced the edge of her ear, swirling in the tiny crevices with a light touch that sent shivers skating down her spine. His hands moved in a slow cadence along the ridges of her spine, fingers playing a silent tune from neck to waist. Her breasts where they pressed into the hard wall of his chest felt heavy and her nipples ached with an intense surge of desire.

The song ended and the music changed to something equally as slow but with the heavy thump of a bass guitar. Ben's hip motion became exaggerated as he shifted in time to the low beat and flutters rippled through the walls of Grace's pussy. More moisture seeped into the crotch of her lace panties. She moved her own hips in concert with his, the ridge of his cock rubbing against her pubic bone. His lips continued their journey around the shell of her ear, then down the column of her neck.

A soft moan floated on the air and Grace realized with a shock it came from her. She wanted Ben to strip her naked and run his tongue over every inch of her body but it appeared he was determined to tease her to a state of unbelievable arousal. He was seducing her in a way no one ever had before. Joe had done the big seduction bit but he'd also been twenty-one years old. Neither of them had come to the relationship with much sophistication or experience. And he hadn't ever practiced this much patience. Youth, she thought. Ben was way past that stage and he was controlling his own desire to give her everything he thought she should have.

"Your husband was young, you said," he murmured in her ear. "Youth is exuberant but lacks experience. I want you to experience it all, Grace. To learn about your own sexuality and understand the gift it is to someone like me."

"Ben." She inhaled slowly and let out a long breath, her heart racing at his words.

"Ssh. Just go with it, Grace. Enjoy it. Open yourself up to it."

He moved his head, tilting it to give him access to the hollow of her throat, where her pulse beat wildly. When his tongue licked gently at the skin, tiny sparks showered through her body. She moaned again, wanted more from him.

"You're incredible," he murmured softly, his lips against her skin. "You set me on fire, Grace. Burn me up alive."

As they continued to sway to the rhythm of the music, Ben's hands moved around between them and slowly unknotted her blouse, letting it fall free. Almost carelessly he tugged up her top, baring her breasts in their fancy lace. His touch on her exposed skin sent those familiar shivers racing through her again. His fingers moved in gentle circles, tracing the lacy edge of her bra, his palms cupping her swollen breasts supported by the thin material.

She kneaded the hard muscles of his back, loving the feel of them as they flexed beneath her touch. With a desperate need to feel his skin, she yanked his shirt from the waist of his jeans, slid her hands beneath the fabric and moved them over his heated skin. And all the while his magic fingers teased at her breasts, pinching the nipples beneath the restraining cups of the bra.

When she thought her breasts would surely explode, his hands dropped to the snap of her jeans. She heard the snick as it opened, then the rasp of the zipper sliding down. Ben's hand rested on her hip, fingertips just inside the top of her panties, branding her skin with their heat.

"Take off your shirt," she whispered, tugging at the material again. "I want to feel your skin against mine."

Ben stopped moving, stepping back barely enough to strip off the shirt, yanked it from his body and tossed it aside. He followed that by disposing of Grace's top and bra. When she felt him skin to skin, her knees weakened and she clutched at his upper arms to steady herself.

Ben brushed his lips against her, a whisper of a caress, then reached for his half-filled champagne glass. With studied care he dripped it one bubble at a time from the hollow of her throat to the valley between her breasts. Setting the glass back down, he followed the trail with his tongue, lapping the liquid, drinking it from her skin.

"Oh god," Grace moaned. "Please, Ben. Please, please, please." Desire was like a thick cloud surrounding her.

"Slow and steady wins the race, darlin'," he crooned.

Grace was sure she'd be one big nerve at the end of a slow race. Unlike the first night they'd been together, Ben was indeed wooing her, seducing her, drawing her into an erotic web she'd never want to find her way out of.

Holding her hips steady with his big, capable hands, Ben sank to his knees, his mouth brushing against the soft skin of her waist and down to the top of her barely there panties. Her fingers dug into his shoulders and she began rocking her pelvis against the heated breath trailing fire across her body. When his hands pushed her jeans down to her ankles she balanced herself to kick them away as quickly as she could.

Ben pressed his face against her through the sheer silk covering her naked cunt and inhaled her scent. Urging her thighs to widen, he swiped his tongue against her wet crotch, his hum of approval vibrating against her and echoing through her body.

Grace didn't know how much longer she could stay upright. One more lick of his tongue and she knew she'd come right where she was standing. Finally he rose and lifted her in his arms, carrying her through the sitting room to the bedroom where he used one hand to tug the covers back. He placed her gently on the silken sheets and kissed her forehead.

"Back in a minute."

When he returned he was carrying the champagne cooler in one hand, the glasses lodged in the ice and the tray of chocolate-covered strawberries in the other. He placed the tray on the bedside table and the cooler in the floor, retrieving the glasses and filling them with the bubbling liquid.

He handed one to Grace, touching the rim of his glass to hers. "May your life always be a sip of champagne, Grace."

The low timbre of his voice set her hormones racing again but not nearly as much as the bright sheen of lust in his eyes. For her. She didn't know what to say so she just sipped at the cold liquid, hoping it would cool her off just a little. Enough so she didn't explode the minute he touched her.

With a flick of a button on the bedside remote, Ben brought the music from the stereo into the bedroom, something sultry and smooth. As the notes drifted on the air he unzipped his jeans and slid them slowly down his hips along with his boxers. His cock sprang free, thick and enormous, rising proudly from the heavy nest of curls. He cradled it in one hand, stroking it slowly as his heated eyes held her gaze.

"Grace." His look was smoldering. "Fucking you is one of the most erotic, most exciting experiences of my life."

"E-Even though I know so much less than your...other women?" The minute the words were out of her mouth she wished them back. How juvenile it sounded.

"Ah but that's what makes it special. With you, darlin', everything is new and fresh and different. Besides," he gave her a wicked grin, "this way I know what we're doing is just for me and I can teach you what to do." The grin disappeared. "Or order you what to do. Would you like that, Grace? For me to give you sexual commands?"

Her heart raced like a high octane engine at the thought. *Yes, yes, yes,* she wanted to shout. And whoever thought that proper Grace Delaney would want to be someone's sexual submissive?

No, not just anyone's. Ben's.

He moved forward onto the bed, positioning himself so he was kneeling between her spread thighs. Reaching over to the nightstand, he lifted one of the strawberries from the tray and stroked it across first one nipple and then the other. Grace's breathing hitched as soft waves of sensation rolled through her.

"Your nipples remind of these strawberries," he told her. "Ripe and plump and juicy."

He leaned forward to feed her the ripe fruit, one bite for her, one for him, the juice trickling down her chin. He licked it off with a soft swipe of his tongue that made her nerves pop with tiny sparks. When it was finished he lifted another piece of fruit from the plate and rubbed the chocolate across one of her nipples. His mouth was hot and wet on her nipples as he sucked at the cool chocolate there. His teeth scraped lightly over the pebbled surface as he took the confection into his mouth.

"Oh my god," she gasped, reaching for his head to pull it close.

He lifted his head and circled her wrists with his fingers. "It's much better when you know you can't touch me," he told her. "When you're spread out like a feast before me and I can take my time." He lowered his voice. "You like it when I restrain you, don't you, Grace?"

She nodded, wordless. She did like everything he did to her. Why had she acted so stupidly the other night?

"I like seeing you helpless, open to my mouth and hands and cock. Does that frighten you, Grace? Is that what made you run away?"

She shook her head and finally the words rushed from her lips. "Honestly? All of it scared me, Ben. The whole scene. But hiding from it hasn't helped. I discovered I really love it all. I *want* it all. With you. Can you imagine what a shock that is to me? I like being wild with you."

His chuckle was low and warm. "Tonight you *will* get it all, darlin'. Every bit and then some." Reaching into the nightstand drawer, he pulled out a pair of handcuffs lined with pink fleece. "I bought these the other day when I had high hopes for the evening. Before you stood me up." A grin played at the corners of his mouth.

"M-Maybe you should punish me for being bad," she ventured, knowing the desire in his eyes was reflected in her own, yet still shocked at her boldness.

His laugh was full and rich. "Oh I think I'll have to do that. But all in its own good time."

He threaded the handcuffs through one of the spindles on the headboard, then locked them around her wrists. His eyes ate her body like a starving man with a glimpse of a bountiful feast. Very slowly he slid her panties down her hips, over her ankles and tossed them to the floor. One warm palm covered her naked pussy.

"Two days and you need shaving again." His voice was husky with need. "If I didn't have other plans for tonight I'd do it right now but we'll put it on the schedule. I love it when there's nothing here between my tongue and your skin."

He knelt between her thighs and ran both large hands over her body, shaping the hills of her breasts, the swell of her tummy, dipping into the creases where thigh and hip joined. His eyes followed the path of his hands, as if memorizing every inch of her.

Grace knew somehow tonight was different from the first time. From all the other times. There was an erotic charge in the air, making everything more…intense, filling her with a desire to hold every minute captive. To savor the delicious taste and feel of him. This was more than just hot, raw sex. This was like falling into a hot pool of sensuality. Of eroticism. And never being able to climb out. She was getting in way over her head again and knew she couldn't do a thing about it. And didn't want to.

He stroked another strawberry across first one nipple, then the other and it was like the feathery touch of brushes against her pebbled tips. The wet heat of his mouth as he licked every drop of the chocolate confection sent lightning bolts of heat stabbing through her directly to her cunt. She wanted to squeeze her thighs together to compress the increased fluttering in the walls of her vagina but his body between her legs kept them wide apart.

Ben took his time, sharing the berries with her before painting the chocolate on the hard tips of her breasts. He was right about the helplessness, except this time it felt different. As if by submitting to him *she* was actually the one in control.

Whoa! What was that all about?

But before she could try to figure out what that meant, Ben was trailing a strawberry down between the valley of her breasts. He paused to upend it at her navel, rubbing the chocolate into the little indentation, then down to the top of her slit. Pressing the tip of the fruit against her clit, he twirled it just enough to send sensations sizzling through her.

His tongue traced the swirl of her bellybutton before his lips pursed over it and sucked the remainder of the chocolate into his mouth before moving his mouth lower. And lower.

"Want to try something a little different, darlin'?" His eyes were heavy-lidded, his voice thick.

"I... You..." She wet her lips with the tip of her tongue. "Like what, exactly?"

He studied every inch of her face. "We've never talked about this." His chuckle was deprecating. "Why would we? This isn't supposed to go anywhere, right? But for the time it lasts, we can make it something special."

She was completely confused. "I don't understand."

"In all your secret reading, sugar, have you read about D/s relationships? About BDSM?"

Her eyes widened and her breath caught in her throat. Oh yes, she'd read all about it. Fantasized about playing the submissive role, her cheeks stained with embarrassment at how wet it made her. How stimulated she became.

How she secretly wished for someone to do those things to her!

She had taken one step forward and two steps backward in this budding relationship with Ben Lowell. Fear and anxiety had trapped her behind the shimmering wall of her desire. Was she ready to take an even bigger step now?

She swallowed hard. "Yes. I have." She felt the blush creep up her cheeks.

"Nothing to be embarrassed about, darlin'." He kissed the tip of her nose. "It can be the most wonderful relationship in the world. Are you game to give it a try? Maybe little baby steps?" He kissed both cheeks. "See what it's like to give up control at the same time realizing you have it more than ever?"

"I don't understand."

"Grace, in a healthy D/s relationship, the Dom's pleasure comes from whatever pleasure the sub gives to him freely. It's built on trust. I'm not suggesting we go the whole nine yards, although I'm convinced with you it would be incredible. But let's just play at it a little, okay? Want to test it out?"

She nodded wordlessly.

He was off the bed in a flash, pulling open the nightstand drawer again and removing three long silk scarves.

"Remember how good it was with the blindfold?" he asked, folding the gossamer material into a wide band.

Grace nodded, watching him.

"We're going to do this again, okay?" he waited for her to nod. "So you can feel absolutely everything. I mean everything, Grace, darlin'."

As soon as the silk was placed across her eyes, she felt herself wrapped in an erotic cocoon. Every nerve ending in her body went on high alert. Her cunt was wet with her liquid and her inner muscles, fluttered, demanded attention. The sound of the music was sharper and Ben humming along with it in a low baritone sent vibrations shuddering through her body.

A threaded knot of tension curled up in her stomach as Ben slipped one of the other scarves beneath her knees, looping the fabric around each of them, lifting them and pulling them wide so he could fasten the long ends to the headboard. Now her entire pussy was exposed for whatever he wanted to do with it. He carefully massaged the muscles of her thighs, hips and calves, slow, patient strokes, testing the muscles for too much strain.

"I want you to enjoy this," he told her. "We never got around to choosing a safe word for you the other night, you know. We need to do it now."

"S-Safe word?" Suddenly she was having second thoughts. Why should she need to be safe from Ben?

He leaned forward and brushed a kiss across her strawberry-tasting lips. "I don't want you ever to be uncomfortable for one minute. This isn't about unrelenting pain. It's about just enough pain to cause unbearable pleasure. About as much variety as we want. So. Any time you want to stop, any time you're uncomfortable, you use that word and everything stops. Got it?"

She nodded. "Rodeo."

"Rodeo?" He huffed a chuckle. "Okay, rodeo it is. Just keep it in the back of your mind." He adjusted her legs and her arms. "Are you okay now?"

"Yes but I'd be better if you touched me."

Another chuckle. "Touched you where, darlin'? Next rule is you always have to tell me where you want my mouth, my tongue, my hands." He paused. "My cock."

She felt heat creep up in her cheeks. That damn blush again. "I want you to touch…my…pussy."

There. She'd said it. Told him what she wanted from him. Needed. Somehow this seemed even bolder than when he'd caught her that first night masturbating and ridden his hands over hers. She waited and when nothing happened she hitched her hips at him, silently urging him to movement.

"Easy," he said, "I'm building a fruit salad here. I like this container better than the one the hotel sent up."

His broad, blunt fingers pressed lightly to separate the lips of her pussy and she felt a small pressure as something move inside her channel.

A strawberry!

The hot walls of her cunt softened the strawberry at its head, allowing the rest of the luscious fruit to move smoothly inside her. He stroked the extended lips of her vulva, then widened her again as a second strawberry followed the first. She wriggled a little, wondering just how many she could take inside, then remembered how long and thick Ben's cock was and relaxed into the unusual stimulation.

"All right now, darlin'. I am going to have myself a real feast. You just lie back and enjoy it."

As if I could do anything else!

Pressing his palms against the insides of her thighs, he widened them even more, then those rough silk lips were brushing over the almost nude lips of her cunt, his tongue outlining their velvety folds before the tip of it entered her vagina and he began to suck out one piece of the plump, juicy berries. The little tiny pebbles on the skin of the fruit were like magic fingers dragging along the tender inner flesh of her pussy, each one like a shock right to her core. The pulse in her womb strengthened, beating its sensual message to the rest of her body.

Restrained as she was and blindfolded so her other senses were heightened, she felt each little movement with great intensity, the muscles of her cunt clutching at the berry as Ben dragged it out with his teeth and sucked it into his mouth. He pressed his lips against her opening as he chewed and swallowed, humming in pleasure, then licked the opening of her pussy with the tip of his tongue before reaching it inside her and pulling the next piece of fruit toward him.

By the time each berry had been sucked out, its juice squirting into her heated pussy, the tiny nubs on it lighting licks of flame along the lining of her vagina, Grace was a shuddering mass of need. Ben was a master at what he was doing, using just the right amount of suction. And all the while his warm finger played a tune on her swollen clit, drawing out and building up her need, while the bass guitar and sax on the CD played a counterpoint that floated on the air.

When the last strawberry had been sucked into his mouth, the juice running down to the crack of her ass, his finger still doing its magic thing with her clit, Ben slipped his stiffened tongue deep into her cunt and brought her to a roaring climax that thundered through her entire body.

Grace felt as if she'd fallen into a sensual whirlpool that kept spinning her around, every tiny muscle and nerve in her body sparking out of control, shivers racing through her as Ben manipulated her clit and her cunt, keeping her hovering at the peak, never letting her down from the grip of the roaring climax that gripped her tightly. At last he withdrew his tongue and languidly lapped her labia and the hot flesh surrounding her clit, his busy fingers slowing their vigorous movements until the last of the shudders and aftershocks had finally faded away.

Chapter Nine

❧

Ben pulled himself farther up on Grace's body, trailing soft kisses along her abdomen. He moved up through the valley of her breasts, pausing at the soft hollow of her throat where her pulse still beat erratically and finally touching his lips to hers.

"Taste yourself." His voice was husky, low. "Taste how your juices mingle with the strawberry. You're delicious, Grace. A meal fit for royalty. And I'm the lucky guy who gets to enjoy this."

She licked his lips with her tongue, enjoying the combined flavors of sweet and tart, which were unbelievably arousing her spent body again.

"I can't," she whispered, wishing she could squeeze her thighs together. "Not again. Not so soon."

He just laughed softly, a possessive sound.

Even when Ben untied the scarves around her knees and stretched her legs out, he kept himself positioned between them, her wet pussy pressed against his chest where the soft pelt covering the hard wall of his chest tickled the sensitive skin.

"Did I hurt you?" he asked in a low voice as his hands massaged her thighs.

Grace shook her head, her limbs still weak, the silk still covering her eyes, every feeling and sensation intensified. "No," she answered and let out a slow breath. "I trust you not to hurt me, Ben. Except in pleasure."

His hands tightened on her reflexively and his lips pressed a kiss at the hollow of her throat. "That's the only kind of pain you should ever have. The sweet edge of it, the kind that makes you hot and aroused. That's what I want to give you, Gracie. All I want is to teach you how to enjoy your body and the things I can make it feel."

"Y-You do." She was still trembling slightly and her words came out unsteadily. "You have no idea how much you do."

He slipped the blindfold from her eyes and kissed each of the lids. Lifting her so she was sitting against the pillows, he took a champagne flute from the nightstand and held it to her lips.

"Drink, darlin'. You deserve nothing but champagne."

She sipped at the liquid which was still cold, the bite of it cool as it slid down her throat. "Um," she said, licking her lips.

"Taste good?"

She nodded.

"I'm going to free your hands from the headboard, Grace, but then tie them behind your back. If that's not okay, tell me now. Remember, you always have your safe word."

"I-It's fine." She licked her lips again. "What do you want me to do?"

He brushed his mouth against hers. "I want you to use these sweet lips on me, Gracie. I want you to be my willing submissive and learn how to give me as much pleasure as I give you." He kissed her again. "I promise you'll enjoy it. Remember how we did it the other night?"

Heat flashed through her body. "Yes." *I loved it. I never thought I would.*

"Tonight I'm going to teach you how to make it even better."

Releasing her wrists from their restraints, he lifted her from the bed and placed her on the floor in front of him, then handcuffed her hands behind her. Grace stared at him,

116

studying his face, pulse pounding as she waited for his next move.

"Kneel," he commanded in a thick heavy voice. "Right in front of me."

She had to work to keep her balance with her hands behind her but she dropped not too awkwardly to her knees on the carpet. His swollen cock was barely an inch from her face. Ben lifted the champagne flute and held it to her lips again.

"Sip slowly, darlin'. Savor it, like I savor the taste of your sweet, sweet cunt."

Grace's head was spinning as the cool, effervescent liquid trickled down her throat.

The music changed again, something smooth and erotic, a counterpoint to the beating of her heart and the racing of her pulse.

Ben cupped one hand under her jaw, using the other to guide his swollen cock to her mouth. Wrapping his fingers around the rigid shaft, he brushed it back and forth against her lips.

"Open your mouth, darlin'," he crooned. "Let me feel those velvet lips on my skin."

Having her hands tied behind her, unable to touch him, only able to do as he ordered, was so arousing it was unbelievable. In the beginning of this…whatever it was…Ben had come at her like a rutting bull and her long dormant sexual needs had responded with the explosion of fireworks. But tonight he was tantalizing her, teasing her, tempting her, drawing her along a voluptuous sensory path unlike anything she'd ever experienced before. She had never felt so worshiped. So cherished.

So alive!

She was excited, nervous, anxious—but definitely ready to try anything Ben had in mind. Whatever this man wanted, she would do it without hesitation.

"Shake your shoulders so I can see your breasts move," he ordered in a thick voice.

Grace did as he asked, her breasts wobbling and her lips clamping tight on Ben's cock to hold it in place.

"God, your breasts are so gorgeous," he breathed. He slipped his hand from her chin to cup one of the swaying mounds, letting his fingertips drift until he could capture a nipple and pinch it. "Gorgeous," he said again. "Spread your knees wider."

Grace spread her knees as much as she could without toppling over and sucked Ben's cock more deeply into her mouth.

"Easy," he whispered. "A little at a time. Let me feel the wetness of your mouth and the slickness of your tongue. Lick me with your tongue, Grace."

She struggled to comply, working her tongue around the thick shaft that nearly filled her mouth completely. She managed to taste the velvety underside, loving the feel of it on her tongue. As Ben increased the pressure on her nipple he worked his penis farther and farther into her mouth. She moaned as the smooth head hit the back of her throat and she felt a tiny drop of semen on the back of her tongue.

"Breathe, sugar," he instructed her. "Breathe so you don't choke. This is a lot for your little mouth to take. We found that out the other night, didn't we?"

She tried to nod her head but she was impaled on his huge spike. Ben kept sliding his cock in and out of her mouth, pushing just a little farther each time, while his fingers tormented her nipple. The pressure on the swollen bud sent fire streaking through her straight to her womb, her pussy quivering as it flooded with her juices.

Grace moved her head faster and faster, pulling back and forth, feeling the pulsing of Ben's cock and the new droplets of semen that fell on her tongue. Without warning, Ben pulled back, gave one last tug on her nipple and lifted her to the bed again, placing her on her knees.

"W-What's wrong?" she stammered. "What did I do?"

"Nothing, sugar." He was breathing heavily as he leaned over her. "I was about ready to come in that sweet mouth of yours but I'd rather come in your ass instead. That lovely, sweet, oh-so-tight ass. That dark hole that no one's ever penetrated before. They haven't, have they, Gracie?"

She shook her head, a dark thrill running through her. "No. No one."

"I am so ready to fuck you, sugar." He ran his fingers through her slit, which she knew had to be dripping. "Oh yeah. Soaked. You love this, don't you, Grace? Every bit of it."

She couldn't speak, only nod.

"I'm going to truly make you mine tonight. Mine. You understand?"

She nodded even as conflicting emotions gripped her. His? Was she ready to belong to someone again? Wait. This was only short-term though, right? He was confusing her but she wanted his cock, his mouth, more than anything, so she nodded her agreement.

"Let's see what we have here," he growled in a low voice as he seated himself and flipped her over his lap. His hardened cock pressed into her as his hand smoothed over the bare skin of her ass.

God, she is every man's wet dream, Ben thought, caressing the cheeks of her ass. Somehow he'd managed to press her On switch and he had no intention of turning it off. There was so much he wanted to teach her about the D/s lifestyle, not just the sex but the trust and give and take of the relationship. He couldn't remember the last time he'd felt this way about a woman. For the first time he began to think about something beyond the next town, the next rodeo, the next woman. He just hoped tomorrow Grace wouldn't run again in fear or anxiety, scared to find out what life could hold for both of them. Especially given his own suddenly confused feelings.

His fingers delved into her cunt again, her copious fluids coating them. She was so responsive. Separating the globes of her buttocks with the fingers of one hand, he used the other to paint her anus with her fluids, pressing just the tip of his finger into her opening. She clenched the cheeks of her ass and without thinking he lifted his hand and brought it down in a sharp slap.

Grace jerked on his lap and he pressed her in place.

"Go with it, Gracie. Let me spank this pretty little ass of yours." He brought his hand down again. "There. Tell me that doesn't make you get even wetter. Hotter." Another slap. "Tell me, Gracie."

"Y-Yes, it does."

"Tell me you like it," he ordered.

"I like it." Her breath came in uneven spurts. "I like it."

"Tell me you love it." Slap, slap. "Beg me to spank you more."

"I-I love it. Oh god." She bit back a sob. "S-Spank me more."

She wriggled on his lap and he realized with heated satisfaction that she was actually rubbing herself on his cock.

Yes!

He wanted to shout the word. Tonight he would definitely make Grace Delaney his. What came next...well, he'd worry about that tomorrow.

Her ass was a nice, warm pink, the flesh quivering, and she was hotter and wetter than ever. The spanking had been an impulse and a chancy one at that. He hadn't meant to push her this far tonight but holy crap, once he got started he couldn't stop. In all his years as a Dom, albeit a low-key one, no woman had ever shredded his self-discipline the way Grace Delaney did. He needed to remember that he was the one in control. He had a responsibility to her to help her enjoy this, not frighten her away.

Turning her, in seconds he had her on the bed on her knees, facing away from him, little moans drifting from her throat. He yanked the pillows forward to prop beneath her and support her. Seeing her helpless like this, hands manacled behind her, legs spread wide, drove him wild.

He pressed one fingertip against the inviting ring of her anus, rubbing it in circles, gentling her. "I promise not to hurt you," he said. "I know this is new for you and I want you to enjoy it."

Next came the gel. He squeezed it onto her opening, then pressed one finger inside, a little at a time. Carefully he spread the lubricant into her tissues, sliding back out then in again in a slow motion. More gel. More stroking of his finger in the hot tunnel. With each stroke of his finger in her ass his cock became even harder and throbbed more heavily, if that was even possible. God, he hoped he could at least wait until he was inside her and not squirt all over her smooth ass cheeks like some teenager with no control.

But the feel of that hot, dark tunnel was driving him wild.

He applied more gel, and this time added a second finger to the first, scissoring them to stretch and soften the virgin hole that beckoned to him. Soft moans rolled from Grace's lips, but he could tell they were sounds of pleasure, not pain. The more he worked her rectum, the louder the sounds became, until finally he was sure she was ready for him, softened enough to take his cock.

His hands were shaking as he grabbed a condom from the nightstand and sheathed himself.

"Here we go, darlin'," he told her. "Take a big, deep breath."

When she did, he pressed against her anus and pushed, slowly and steadily, until he was fully seated inside her before exploding and embarrassing himself.

Oh god!

He closed his eyes and gritted his teeth, holding onto his control by a very fragile thread.

He began to pump into her, slowly at first, then faster and faster. His fingers dug into her hips, holding her in place as he plundered that clasping, dark tunnel, the heat scorching him. The sight of her propped up by the pillows, hands manacled behind her, drove him even higher. He kept his upper body straight, using his hands on her hips as leverage. Stabilized by the pillows, her body soon began to thrust back against him, her ass hitting his thighs, as her orgasm began to unwind through her body.

"Not yet," he gasped. "Do not come yet."

"Please," she begged. "Oh please."

Ben closed his eyes, focusing only on her body and its grip on his cock. When he felt the tingling in his back and the tightening of his balls, he thrust harder, faster.

There it was.

Yes!

"Now," he shouted. "Come now."

They fell over the edge of the cliff together, her body jerking back against him as his cock pulsed over and over again in her rectum. Skin slapped against skin and her mewling sounds mingled with his hoarse cries. Lights burst behind his eyes, electricity crackled around him. He wanted to stay in the hot grip of that dark tunnel forever, swallowed up by it, connected to her in the most intimate way.

He thought he owned her? God! The truth was, *she* owned *him*.

He pulled her as tightly to him as he could, feeling her muscles contract and spasm, until the last bit of cum had pulsed into the latex reservoir.

And then it was done.

Finished.

He fumbled for the release on the handcuffs, freeing her wrists, then collapsed forward on her, catching his weight on his forearms. His heart hammered so hard he thought it would break his ribs. The music drifting from the stereo was a counterpoint to gasping breath as they struggled to drag air into their lungs.

Ben had no idea how long they lay there, limp and spent. He managed to rouse long enough to dispose of the condom but the effort a shower would require seemed beyond both of them. He dragged the covers over them, curled his body around hers and in seconds they were both asleep.

* * * * *

Grace woke in the morning, pleasantly sore in places she didn't know had nerves, her body humming with satisfaction. A warm male body was curled around her, one muscular arm lying against her tummy, one hand cupping a breast. Something hard and thick prodded at her rear, which was unusually tender. Like instant replay, the night's activities came back to her, forcing a blush that rose though her entire body.

"Mornin', sugar."

The deep voice resonated against the nape of her neck, follow by the tiny lick of a tongue and a gentle nip.

Grace tried to bury her face in the pillow but Ben slid his hand up to cup her chin, refusing to allow her to hide from him.

"Grace?" He nipped at her ear. "Don't turn away from me. Last night was fantastic. I want you to embrace it, not regret it."

She didn't know what to say. Regret was the last word she'd use to describe it but she didn't want Ben to think she was—

"Stop," he said. "I know what you're thinking." He tugged at her body until she faced him. "What we did was good, Gracie. Outstanding. I know everything was new and beyond your experience but you gave me the gift of yourself. I'll never abuse that. Ever. You were magnificent."

"I've never..." She could hardly get the words out, a phrase she seemed to use more than ever these days.

"Been fucked in the ass?" He smiled at her. "I know that. It's why it's such a gift." He smacked her lightly on her buttocks. "Right now, though, we need a shower. Badly. Then food."

"Oh my god." She tried to sit up. "What time is it? I have to get to the office."

"Grace, Grace, Grace." He tugged her more tightly to him, his hand drifting along the curve of her hip, the swell of her buttocks. "Don't look at the clock. Not today. How about just for one day you play hooky. Tell everyone to bag it and have fun."

She had never missed a day of work in her uptight life except when she was sick. She felt the weight of responsibility dragging on her, the ever-present schedule, the demands of clients and of her staff. Her body tensed as it all ran through her mind.

"Shut off your brain, sugar," Ben crooned. "Just for today go with the flow. Come on, Grace. The rodeo's only in town for another four days. Let's make the most of it."

Her stomach knotted. Four days. She'd almost forgotten. And of course that would be the end of this. He'd made that very clear from the beginning. Last night he'd claimed her in a very possessive manner but she realized she was his only until the last horse trailer pulled out of San Antonio.

But hadn't that been what she wanted too? The thought of a long-term relationship with someone like Ben, someone so masculine and sexual and overpowering, scared the pants off her. But after all her years of rigid discipline, didn't she deserve a little fun? Just for one moment out of time?

Letting out a slow breath, feeling as if she was facing a visit to the principal's office, she nodded her head. "A-All right. I will."

His grin was so wide it nearly split his face. "You'll do it? Hot damn." He smacked her rear end lightly again. "Let's get to it then."

The shower might have taken less time if they hadn't decided to bathe each other. That led to some erotic playtime and by the time Ben had finished bringing her to orgasm twice with his fingers, Grace wasn't sure she'd be able to set foot outside the suite. She was glad he had ordered a big breakfast for them. She usually had little more than a toasted bagel and coffee but today she needed calories to replenish her body.

Showered and dressed, she dug out her cell phone and nervously called her office.

"You aren't coming in?" Joyce sounded as startled as if Grace had told her she was going to dance naked in the street. "B-But you always check everything out before the weekend and today's Friday. And you have two appointments this afternoon. What shall I do with them?"

Grace ignored the tiny knot of apprehension in her stomach. Ben was right. She had good people working for her and she needed to use them. "Give one to Rita and the other to Jim. They're both very capable of handling them."

There was a pause at the other end of the conversation. "Grace, are you all right?" Then Joyce squeaked with excitement. "Oh wait. It's the hunk, isn't it? All right!" Grace imagined her secretary pumping her fist in the air. "You go, girl. I'll handle things here."

Grace snapped her cell phone shut, a rueful grin playing on her lips. "My secretary must think I'm a repressed virgin," she told Ben. "She practically told me to let it all hang out. Or don't they use that expression anymore?"

Ben laughed. "It doesn't matter. It fits the situation." He lifted the cell phone from her hand and put it on the table next to the couch. "This stays here today. No work. Only play."

"But what if someone calls?" she protested.

"That's what they have voice mail for, sugar." He guided her out the door. "Fun, Grace. Remember?"

A new concept but suddenly she felt as if a weight were lifted from her shoulders. She was going to do something naughty, something forbidden. She was going to spend the day having *fun*.

From the hotel they took the stairs down to the famed Riverwalk. The day was perfect, just warm enough with puffy clouds in a brilliant blue sky and the sun hanging suspended like a giant golden ball. The breeze was just enough to counteract the heat from the sun. If they'd ordered up a special day it couldn't have been any better.

They took their time strolling along the walkway that wound in front of an eclectic mix of shops and restaurants, taking their time, mingling with the tourists, the residents and the business crowd taking a moment to lunch in the open air or entertain a client in an exceptional setting. When Ben slipped his hand into hers and laced their fingers together it gave her a giddy feeling.

Why don't I ever do this? Oh, well, because who would I do it with?

Like with everything else in her life, she'd established a narrow routine and never varied from it.

Ben insisted on taking her into a western wear shop and buying her two outfits that she didn't think she'd ever wear again once he left. But he was so quietly in control it didn't even occur to her to object or protest. She felt as if she were in an alternate universe and the real Grace Delaney was actually plodding away in her office putting tiny numbers into tiny squares.

She blushed when he came back from the lingerie section with tiny little scraps of silk that would barely cover her cunt and her breasts.

"B-Ben," she stuttered, "you can't…I mean…"

He winked at her. "Gotta have new panties to go under the new clothes, right?"

She was still blushing when she finally put the outfit on. The jeans, tighter than anything in her closet, fit her like a second skin, outlining every crevice of her body. Sheer blouses covered low-cut tank tops that left little to the imagination. When she moved the little pin to the outfit she had on, she felt a warmth spread through her and she wondered for a moment if she was actually glowing.

Ben grinned at her as she stared at herself in the mirror.

"Maybe I made a mistake here. I'll be fighting other men off with a stick when they see you in these clothes."

Her cheeks heated. "Ben, I really can't go out in clothes like this," she told him.

He cocked an eyebrow. "Why not? You'll be the most gorgeous woman out there. Every female will want to scratch your eyes out, they'll be so jealous."

She laughed. "You make everything sound so…okay."

Ignoring the obviously staring sales clerk, he cupped her face and kissed her breathless. "It *is* okay, Gracie. All of it."

He insisted she wear one of the outfits and she couldn't help stopping now and then in front of a shop, checking herself out in the window reflection as if she didn't recognize herself.

Well, I don't. But I think I like this new Grace better than I thought I would.

When they stopped for a drink at an outdoor café she realized Ben's prediction was completely accurate. The women who walked by, smart-looking women with expensively styled hair and impeccable makeup, stared daggers at her. Especially with Ben lounging back in the chair next to her, a possessive arm around her shoulders.

Grace couldn't remember the last time she'd felt so free, so loose. She couldn't decide if it was the utterly erotic experience of the previous night, Ben's possessive presence or the three margaritas she consumed. Or a combination of all three. But by the time they stopped for an early dinner, she was shocked to realize she hadn't thought of the office once.

"I like to eat early on the nights I ride," Ben told her. "I hope you don't mind. And I eat light. But don't let that stop you from ordering whatever you want." He winked at her. "You'll need your energy for later."

She was chowing down on an enchilada platter at an outdoor table of a well-known Mexican restaurant when a nasal voice broke into her concentration.

"Why, Grace Delaney, is that you in that outrageous outfit?"

She nearly choked on her bite of food as she looked up at the tall blonde standing beside their table. Anita Sandler. Bitch of the world. A client Grace had inherited when the woman's much-older husband died and left her with more money than was sensible. Even the steep fee she charged wasn't enough to make up for the constant headache the woman gave her.

She set down her fork and dabbed at her mouth with her napkin. "Hello, Anita. Nice to see you."

Anita's eyes raked over every visible inch of her body. "That outfit's a little out of your usual wardrobe, isn't it?"

And could your voice be more catty?

"I picked it out myself," Ben said, rising from his chair. "Gorgeous outfit for a gorgeous woman, don't you think?" he held out his hand. "Ben Lowell."

Grace watched Anita's predatory gaze take in every inch of the man in front of her.

"Well. Aren't you the surprise. Grace, I didn't know you'd been keeping such a hunk so well hidden."

"Actually I'm the one doing the hiding," Ben said. "I like to keep Grace all to myself." He touched the brim of his Stetson. "Nice to meet you. Don't let us keep you from whatever you're doing."

Anita's face turned a mottled shade of red. "Well. Nice to meet you too. I guess." She grabbed Ben's hand again. "I insist Grace bring you to my next party." She turned back to Grace again. "I'll make sure your invitation went out."

I'm sure you will, Grace thought sarcastically.

"Thanks for the invitation." Ben gave her a polite smile. "We'll think about it."

Gathering her dignity around her, Anita tottered off on her wedge-heel sandals, back stiff, head high as she tossed her shiny brown hair.

Grace stared after her, open-mouthed. "I've never been to any of her parties, Ben."

He chuckled. "I guessed as much. I've met more women like Anita than you can imagine. Man-eaters. You know what I say about them? Use 'em and lose 'em."

She tilted her head. "And what do you say about me, Ben Lowell?"

A slow, lazy, almost predatory grin transformed his face. "I say you are the hottest woman I've ever taken to bed and I can't wait to do it again. That you're special and I'm the luckiest man alive that you chose me to step out of character with."

She knew she was blushing but couldn't help it. Ben reached across and lifted her free hand, taking it to his mouth where he pressed a light kiss on her knuckles. He didn't say anything. The kiss said it all. Then he winked at her and went back to his food.

"Will I be able to get in tonight to see you ride?" Grace asked as they were lingering over coffee. "Are there still tickets left? The last time I looked they had a Sold Out sign up."

"I'm taking you in with me tonight," he told her. "Giving you a chance to see what it's like backstage, so to speak."

"Really?" She realized she was squeaking but excitement coursed through her. The lure of the behind-the-scenes mystique was powerful.

Ben's warm chuckle rumbled in his chest. "Yes, really. You just have to be very careful and do exactly what I tell you to."

"No problem. Absolutely." She clapped her hands together. "Oh this is terrific. I feel as if I'm going to see the real Ben Lowell."

His face was suddenly serious. "The real me is the one you were with last night, Grace. And the one with you today. The rodeo is just how I make my living these days."

"To get enough money to buy that ranch," she said, her voice sober.

He nodded. "That's right. Just keep remembering that. Okay?"

"Okay." She grinned impishly. "But I can still cheer for you, right?"

"I wouldn't have it any other way." He signaled for the check. "We'd better get going. I like to have plenty of time to check my rigging and see where I am in the order of competitors. And I need to spend some time with Hotshot too. I made arrangements for him to be fed and watered but he and I need our quiet time together."

"You talk about him as if he's human," Grace commented as they made their way back to the stairs to street level.

"Sometimes I think he is. When I introduce you to him, you'll see what I mean."

Chapter Ten

ℬ

Grace fell in love the minute they stepped through the back door of the arena to the area where the animals were kept. One long section was divided into stalls for horses, while another held the bulls that had been specially bred for competition and the calves for the roping and cutting events. The area on both sides of the arena had metal bar fencing set up, sections locked together in the required configurations. Grace noticed both hallways led directly to the arena where a system of pens had been set up.

"Those are the chutes," Ben told her, following her gaze. "That's where the calves are herded before being let loose into the ring, where the riders wait for the gate to open and where they bring each bull or bronc for the rider to mount up."

Grace tried to take in as much of the explosion of noise and color and movement as she could. Watching the activity around her, she could see how the rodeo life could easily get into someone's blood. The sights, the sounds, the aromas. The magnificent animals, everything from the horses to the little calves used in the roping events. The sizzle of adrenaline in the air.

Every place she looked people were moving in what looked like chaos but she realized was actually some kind of choreographed dance, where everyone knew their place and their steps. Unlike the people in the big room where the food was sold, these people—both men and women—were in worn jeans, t-shirts or shirts with the sleeves rolled up past their elbows and scuffed boots that had seen a lot of wear.

"These are the workers who make the rodeo operate," Ben continued. "Most of them are former rodeo competitors who retired for one reason or another. Their experience gives them a good understanding of what needs to be done to make things work."

"I don't see any of the other riders back here," she told him, looking around.

He chuckled. "There's a lot of us here but everyone leaves their fancy duds in their lockers while they prep for the evening's events."

Grace inhaled the mingled scents of animals, humans, straw and leather, the aroma stirring her blood like some exotic cologne. She felt the same whisper of excitement that had streaked through her the first time she'd been to the circus, or seen the famous Lipizzaner horses perform.

"Oh Ben." She turned to him, clutching his arm. "This is fantastic. No wonder you love this life so much."

He laughed at her enthusiasm. "You might think differently if you were on the back of one of those mad bulls, or chasing disobedient calves. Or riding an ornery bronc trying to buck you off."

"I've never even ridden a horse," she admitted shyly.

"No? Maybe we'll come down here during the day and I can give you a slow walk on Hotshot. We'll see." He grabbed her hand. "Come on. I have to get busy."

They wound their way through groups of people, many of them nodding to Ben, smiling or waving hello as they moved down the walkway between the horse stalls. Halfway down the row they stopped at a stall where a horse peeked over the stall gate, big eyes watching them with curiosity. As soon as Ben approached, he nickered softly and rubbed muzzle against the man's palm.

"Hey, boy," Ben said softly. "Got someone here for you to meet. If you treat her nicely, you might get a little treat." He reached out and drew Grace closer. "This is Grace and she's someone pretty special to me. Say hello to her."

The horse bobbed his head up and down and made the same noise he'd greeted Ben with.

Grace laughed with delight. "You're right. He thinks he's a person."

"Go ahead," Ben urged. "Reach out slowly and rub his forehead. He loves it."

Grace extended her hand tentatively and when the horse pushed his head against her palm and made a small noise of satisfaction, she relaxed and rubbed the mottled skin.

"He's a sweetheart," she cried. "I don't think I've ever seen one with a spotted coat like this."

The horse, big and with a broad conformation, had a leopard-spotted coat, white and roan, with large white circles around his eyes.

Ben fished a cube of sugar from his pocket and held it out to Hotshot on his open palm. "He's an Appaloosa. The Nez Perce Indians used them and the breed almost died out when most of them were slaughtered at the end of the Nez Perce War."

"But that's terrible." Grace was shocked at something so senseless.

"No kidding. But there were a few left and some dedicated people worked very hard to regenerate the breed. Because they are so big and strong they make excellent cutting horses and are used a lot in ranch work."

"So he'll go to Wyoming with you?" She hated to think of that. Ben would leave, finish the current rodeo circuit, then head northwest and she'd probably never see him again. Telling herself it was all for the best didn't help one bit. How had she let her defenses down this way, so he'd somehow become more than just a wild fling, something she'd have to get over quickly?

"Absolutely. I'm counting on him to set an example for the other horses I'll need to train." He rubbed Hotshot's muzzle. "Right, boy?" He turned back to Grace. "We've been through a lot together, Hotshot and me. I guess we'll finish going down the road together."

Ben opened the gate and walked into the stall, urging the horse back away from the opening, then running his hands over him, checking him for any scrapes or other areas of injury. He checked the horse's hooves and fetlocks, running his hands over his legs.

"Sometimes he gets a little too rambunctious out in the arena," Ben explained. "He collects some 'souvenirs' that don't show up until the next day. But he seems just fine." Closing the gate again, he tugged Grace farther down the corridor with him. "I need to check and see what time my events are tonight and where I am in the lineup."

"What are you riding in tonight?"

"Hotshot and I are in the calf roping. Then I'm in the bull riding semifinals."

"Semifinals?"

"Yeah. The top eight make it to the finals two nights from now," he went on.

Grace's stomach dropped. She'd seen Ben twice on those angry monsters and both times she'd held her breath until he was safely off and away.

"And then?" She felt idiotic knowing so little about the thing that really shaped this man standing next to her. This is what he was a product of and now she was trying to understand it so she could place him more comfortably in her mind.

And making things too complicated, idiot. Just enjoy yourself. Now and...later.

He shrugged. "We'll talk about that when it happens. Right now I'm focusing on tonight."

"I think I'm afraid to watch you on the bulls," she confessed. "They're so...big and, oh, I don't know, angry."

"That's the way they're bred," he explained. He put his arm around her and drew her close. "I won't tell you it's safe," he said, "but it's as safe as the rodeos can make it. They have spotters watching and the clowns that distract the bulls are very well trained."

Just the same, Grace couldn't control an involuntary shiver.

"Come on," Ben said. "I'll introduce you to the handlers. These guys know what they're doing, believe me."

Danny Perez was checking the setup of the pens, giving orders to a crew as to how he wanted them placed and checking all the locking mechanisms. He looked to be at least fifty years old, tall and lean and weathered, with a blinding smile.

"Danny rodeo'd for fifteen years," Ben said by way of introduction. "Then decided to help the rest of us still getting our brains beat out. He's extra good with the bulls."

"Pleased to meet you." He stuck out his hand and Grace shook it, feeling its hard and calloused surface.

"I heard you talking," he said. "These bulls are specially bred by rodeo stockmen, who do nothing else. Most of them are former rodeo riders too. The rodeos contracts with them and they move the stock from show to show."

"The animals buck because they don't like the weight of the rider on their backs," Ben added. "The flank strap," he picked one up from a nearby rail and held it up, "exerts pressure like a saddle girth but doesn't hurt the bulls at all."

Danny's grin split his weathered face. "And your man here is one of the best riders I've ever seen. You don't need to worry about him."

She started to tell Danny that Ben was only hers temporarily but decided it would involve too much explanation. Instead, she followed Ben to where the program sheet for the night was tacked up on a bulletin board. His events were fourth and seventh and he was the fifth entrant in each of them.

Next he led her into a tack room, to a section with his name in a slot, where he checked his gear. And finally they ended up in a locker room where he checked his boots, spurs and the outfit he'd wear that evening. She noticed a belt hanging on a hook with a wide buckle and asked about it.

"Won the buckle at the Nationals in Las Vegas." He said it in an offhand manner, as if it didn't really matter.

"But that's incredible." Grace reached out her hand and ran her fingers over the engraved metal. "Why don't you wear it more often? I thought... I mean according to Melanie this is a really big deal."

He snorted. "Melanie would certainly think so. She's a charter member of the buckle bunnies club."

"But—"

"Forget it, Grace. I'm not like the guys who wear it day and night. It just meant a big paycheck to me. That's all."

Case closed.

"Want some coffee?" He looked at his watch. "We've got a little time before I have to get ready."

"Sure. That would be nice."

They wound their way through the maze to a back door into the main food area. Just like the first night Grace had been there, the place was jammed and the level of conversation filled the air. People were laughing, talking, shouting back and forth to each other. Grace was waiting while Ben paid for their coffee when she heard someone call her name.

"Grace? Honey, is that you?"

She turned to find Melanie Keyes hurrying toward her. Much as she loved the woman, she also sensed a third degree coming. She sighed.

"Hi, Melanie."

Help me, Ben.

Melanie slid her glance toward Ben. "I see you decided to take my advice."

Grace tried to figure an easy way out of this but Ben turned just at that moment.

"If your advice was to spend her time with me," he drawled, "then you have my thanks." He handed Grace one of the coffee cups. "You'll have to excuse us. We have some things to do before my first event."

He put his arm around Grace and guided her through the mob to the door they'd used to enter.

"Thank you," she breathed, when he closed it behind him.

"I didn't think you were in the mood to play Twenty Questions with Melanie. I sure wasn't. I thank her for introducing us but the rest of it…" His voice trailed off.

"Belongs to us," she finished. She wished she knew what *the rest of it* actually was. Then she mentally shook herself. *Enjoy it now,* she reminded herself. *You don't want any more out of this than he does.* Ben Lowell was not the kind of man she could handle long-term. Short-term was enough of a struggle.

Deliberately she brushed stray thoughts from her mind, determined that nothing would damage the warm, relaxed mood of the day.

Ben watched the first couple of events with her in the staging area. They stood well to the side of the activity, leaning on metal fencing, listening to the crowd roar and applaud. Ben gave her a thumbnail history of each entrant and explained the rules of the events. It was a lot different from watching from a seat in the arena.

"I could get addicted to this," she told him.

He hugged her gently. "Just make sure you don't get addicted to another rodeo cowboy."

"Fat chance," she told him. "I can barely handle the one I've got."

Then it was time for Ben to get ready. He turned Grace over to Danny who found her a seat perched on a metal fence, out of harm's way but still with a view of the arena. She barely paid attention to what was going on as she kept her eyes on the place where Ben would enter on Hotshot.

And there he was, in jeans, hand-tooled boots and a western shirt with a cowboy twirling a lariat embroidered on it. She could tell at once he was completely focused on what he was about to do so she mentally blew him a kiss, not wanting to distract him.

He led Hotshot into the pen, waiting for the announcement, the bell to ring and the gate to open. When it did he flew into the arena, chasing the calves that had been turned loose from another pen. He was fluid grace, he and the horse moving as one as he twirled the rope, let it fly and watched it drop over the horns of a calf. Hotshot pulled up at once, Ben leaped from the saddle, bound the calf's hooves with the rope as required, then raised his hands to show he was finished.

Grace didn't know much about times but from the cheer that went up when Ben's was announced she gathered he'd done very well. Danny turned to her from his place hanging on a rail and grinned.

"Your man's in first place so far. He could win big points tonight."

"What happens then?" she asked.

"He gets tonight's purse plus he carries those points to the Nationals in Las Vegas." He winked. "Lots of bucks there."

And another step closer to his ranch.

She tried not to fidget waiting for the bull riding. She knew she wouldn't see Ben before the event was called. He'd be in the back, away from distractions, gathering himself for the ride. Danny kept checking on her to make sure she was all right and she gave him reassuring smiles.

When the bull riding was announced Grace could almost feel the adrenaline level rise in the arena. Bodies shifted, tension wrapped itself around everyone and the crowd seemed to hold a collective breath.

Grace found she was holding hers too. Her fingers inadvertently tightened into fists and she stared again down the corridor, watching for Ben to come striding forward. She barely paid attention to the first four contestants, although the snorting and pawing of each bull as he was led into the chute awaiting the rider made butterflies tumble in her stomach.

And then he was there, his long, lean muscular body nothing less than coiled energy, his eyes focused on the stomping bull Danny and another man were readying.

When Ben climbed onto the side rails of the chute, she reminded herself he'd been doing this for a long time and knew exactly how to handle himself. She held her breath as he readied himself to take his place on the animal stomping the ground below him. With the men on either side assisting him, he lowered himself onto the broad back of the bull, wound the rope around his hand and flexed his other fist. Then he nodded, one of the men signaled to the announcer, the gate flew open and the bull charged out onto the dirt floor, doing his best to dislodge Ben from his back.

Grace held her breath, nearly biting through her bottom lip as she watched him hang on for the ride, one arm out as required, legs moving in a familiar rhythm she'd seen the other bull riders use. He was poetry in motion, a symphony of grace, totally in control despite the bull's best efforts. It was easy to see why he'd won so many events. Excitement raced through her body. Her nipples throbbed and moisture flooded her crotch. How could she be so turned on just watching a man riding a bull?

She was sure it was the longest eight seconds she'd ever lived through. When the bell rang, Ben threw himself from the bull, rolling and landing on his feet, careful to keep away from the flying hooves. The rodeo clowns raced into the arena and did their thing to distract the animal until he could be contained.

When Ben's score was announced the audience screamed and stamped its feet, the noise filling the arena and echoing off the high ceiling.

"He's got the best time," Danny yelled to her. "He's the only one who lasted the full eight seconds plus he didn't lose points in style. He did it just right. He'll be in the finals. And he's gonna win. You bet your ass."

A combination of fear and exhilaration raced through Grace's blood. She leaped off her perch, nearly falling to the dirt floor.

Ben was grinning like an idiot when he walked through the gate to the safety area. Grace waited for Danny and the others to shake his hand and clap him on the back. Then she launched herself at him with total exuberance. Before she could even think about what she was doing, she wrapped her arms around his neck and her legs around his waist and kissed him as hard as she could, ignoring the dirt and sweat on his face.

His hard arms tightened around her, holding her close, and he deepened the kiss despite the yelling and hooting mob around him.

"I have lots of energy to work off tonight," he murmured, sliding his mouth to her ear. "Are you up to it?"

Her heart was hammering against her ribs like a runaway locomotive, the extra surge of adrenaline propelling erotic images through her brain. Ben too was reacting as the thick ridge of his cock pressed against her through his clothing. She tilted her head back slightly and the look in his eyes nearly singed her skin.

"Oh yeah, cowboy," she breathed softly. "Bring it on."

He licked the edge of her ear. "Later."

He lowered his arms to let her slide down the length of his body and she felt every inch of his hardness. When she

Rodeo Heat

heard the chuckles and wolf whistles she looked around and realized more than a dozen people were standing around them, watching her and Ben intently. The heat of embarrassment crept up her cheeks and she lowered her gaze.

Ben tilted her chin up. "It's okay, sugar. They're all friends of mine."

He put his arm around her and tucked her in close to him as he continued to accept congratulations from people walking up to him. Grace noted four or five heavily made-up females in tight denims and low-cut blouses eyeing her with a mixture of envy and resentment and swallowed her grin.

Too bad. He's mine, at least for now.

The rest of the bull riders finished their turns, shaking Ben's hand as the event ended and his time still held at the best. The next event was called and Ben whispered to Grace, "We can get out of here now. Just give me a minute to change."

Danny came up behind them. "I'll take care of the lady and see she gets to the door," he told Ben. "You come back to this area and you'll never get out of here."

"Thanks, Danny." He kissed Grace lightly on the lips. "See you in five."

"This way," Danny said, ushering Grace away from all the activity to a chair by the rear door Ben always used. "You know, I never thought I'd see Ben let any female put a rope on him."

"Oh no," Grace protested. "You've got it all wrong. Ben and I are just...enjoying ourselves while he's here in San Antonio. That's all."

Danny studied her face. "Yeah, you can say that if you want to but I've known Ben too long. This is more than buckle bunny bingo to him." He paused as if searching for the right words. "Ben's a lot of man for a woman to handle, you know."

A tiny frisson of panic danced over Grace's skin. How much did Danny know about Ben's sex life? About his sexual preferences? Was that what he was referring to? Then she mentally shook her head. No, Ben would never discuss intimate details like that with anyone. That much she was sure of. No, this was just an acknowledgement of the alpha male that Ben obviously was.

Grace smiled. "I know. And we're good, Danny. Thanks."

"No problem." He turned as the sound of boot heels approached. "And here's the man now."

Grace stood up as Ben approached and held out his hand to her

"Thanks," he told Danny. "See you Sunday night."

"You won't be here tomorrow night?" Grace asked as they headed toward his truck.

"Nope." He opened the passenger door for her. "I don't compete again until the last night. That's when the finals are for each event and the prize money and points are awarded."

"So what will you do until then?" she asked as he climbed into the cab of the truck beside her.

He looked over at her and gave her a heated smile. "I'm hoping you'll help me pass the time."

Did he mean for her to stay with him until then? Could she do it? Leave herself with no space to retreat if she needed to?

Ben picked up her hand and kissed her knuckles. "Don't overthink it, Grace. Just go with it. I know it's a stretch for you not to run back to your house every night. I'd tell you okay, take me with you but that's a boundary we don't seem able to cross. You want to keep things separate? Okay. But Monday I'll be gone, so let's not waste any time between now and then."

Gone? Her stomach pitched and she swallowed hard.

Well, stupid, isn't that what you want? A fling with no strings? An erotic journey that you know has an end? A time when you can go back to being controlled, organized Grace? So what's the

harm in staying with him until then? Monday you can walk back into your life. Just like you want.

Right?

"Grace?" His voice broke into her thoughts. "You're making me a little nervous here."

She let out a slow breath. "Of course I'll stay with you. Besides, we have to celebrate your big night."

He laughed, a deep warm sound. "I'm hoping Sunday night we'll have even more to celebrate." He kissed her hand again. "Okay, darlin'. I can't wait to get to the party. Tonight's all about pleasure, Grace. Of every kind."

* * * * *

They barely exchanged a word riding up in the elevator. The sexual heat between them, the sense of anticipation, filled the small space completely. Grace was sure if they touched each other the elevator car would spontaneously combust and there were two other couples occupying the space with them.

When they reached Ben's floor one of the couples also got off, so Grace and Ben walked as sedately to his suite as they could. She swallowed a grin as he fumbled with the lock, needing three tries to get the keycard to finally work.

But once inside he slammed the door shut and pushed her up against it with his body. His mouth was hot and greedy as it captured hers, his tongue tasting her lips and teeth before sweeping inside to drink from her as if he'd never have a taste again. His lean fingers threaded through her hair, tilting her head to give him better access, a better angle. His tongue was everywhere, igniting nerves in the sensitive skin and currents of electricity shooting straight to her cunt.

Grace pressed her hands against his back, feeling the hard muscle there, the honed body of a man who'd been doing what he did for a long time. The heat of his skin radiated through the smooth fabric of his shirt, scorching her hands and raising her own body heat even more. The thick, hard ridge of his cock pressed against the softness of her belly, the denim of his pants doing little to restrain it. Her panties, already wet, became soaked with a new flood of moisture and her nipples were as hard as diamonds, aching for the feel of his hands and his mouth.

Impatiently Ben pulled up her blouse and tank top and shoved her bra out of the way. His fingers pinched and tugged at her throbbing nipples, squeezing them until she moaned with the pleasure of it. Hands unsnapped her jeans and pushed them along with her panties down to her ankles. Somehow they disposed of her boots while Ben unzipped his fly, freeing his cock and scrabbled in his wallet for a condom.

His palms cupped the cheeks of her ass as he hoisted her to the right level, drew back slightly and plunged into her, seating himself with one hard thrust. Grace felt as if every empty space in her body was filled to capacity. Pleasure speared through her, pulses throbbed and the muscles of her pussy gripped Ben's penis like a vise.

"Fuck me," she breathed, shocking herself as the words popped from her mouth. But the excitement of the backstage area of the rodeo, the mingled aromas of sweat and animal flesh, the thrill of danger all combined to drive her into a high state of arousal.

"You bet I'll fuck you," Ben breathed in her ear. "I'll ride you like one of those wild bulls, only you won't be able to buck me off. Come on, Grace, ride with me."

He pulled back slightly then thrust again, hips setting up a hard rhythm. With every push he drove deeper, harder and Grace could do nothing but hang on for dear life. Her orgasm rose and broke over with her no warning, shaking her like a leaf tossed in the wind. She was mindless, convulsing, impaled on the hard thickness of his shaft, her spasms milking him as he emptied himself with great spurts into the thin shield of the latex.

"Jesus, Grace." Ben leaned his forehead against hers. "What the hell just happened?"

Grace struggled for enough breath to speak. "I think you…we…I mean…"

"You mean I fucked your brains out? Darlin', that was more like a world-class explosion." He dragged air into his lungs. "I don't know how the hell we're still breathing." He lowered her gently to her feet and scattered kisses on her face.

"I think it was the night," she whispered, her heart still hammering. "All that testosterone, all that male action. And those magnificent animals."

His grin was shaky. "Do you include me in those magnificent animals?"

She smiled back at him. "Without a doubt."

"I think we need to get rid of the rest of these clothes," he told her as he proceeded to do just that. When they were completely naked, he took her hand and led her toward the bathroom. "Shower. I can't believe you didn't smack me and make me wash off all that sweat and animal smell first."

She laughed, a soft sound. "I think it was an aphrodisiac, if you want the plain, unvarnished truth. I can't believe what came over me." Warmth crept up her face. "I've never done anything like that before."

"I think the list of those things is growing, isn't it?"

They were in the bathroom now, Ben disposing of the condom while pulling a fresh one out of the vanity drawer and turning on the shower heads. It suddenly occurred to Grace how badly she needed a shower, perspiration coating her skin and the liquid of her arousal glistening on her thighs.

Ben adjusted the spray to his satisfaction then led Grace inside, reaching for the soap and handing it to her. "Wash me, Grace. Lather me all over."

She raised her eyes to his face, the look the same as the one he'd worn the night before when he began her introduction into the roles of Dominant/submissive. Hot, hard, avaricious. Greedy, as if he'd devour her any moment. And caring, as if she were a precious gem.

Conflicting emotions battled each other inside her shaky body but the thought of refusing him didn't even enter her head. The thought that startled her was how turned on she was by the whole idea. Who was she turning into?

She held out a slim hand for the soap and began to work up a lather in her palms. Applying the suds in a circular motion, she reached up and worked her way across his chest to his shoulders, then down his granite-hard arms. When she smoothed her hands across his chest, she paused to tease his flat nipples and rake her fingernails across the surrounding areolas. Ben sucked in his breath and the muscles in his stomach tightened.

"Lower," he commanded.

Grace swept her hands down over his navel and the taut muscles of his abdomen until she reached his cock, already swollen and pulsing again in readiness.

"Stroke it." His voice was harsh with need. "Take it in your hands and rub it up and down. Let me feel you do it."

Grace's hands were slick as she obeyed, stroking his cock from root to tip and back again, rubbing her soap-covered thumb across the velvety head.

"Now my balls," Ben told her, his fingers wrapping lightly around her wrist, moving her hand downward as he widened his stance.

Grace knelt in front of him and massaged the soap into the lightly haired skin, feeling the hardness of his testicles rolling beneath her fingertips. He jerked slightly as she increased the pressure and her hand brushed the inside of his thigh.

"That's enough." He pulled her hand away, his voice thickening with desire. "Now my legs."

She soaped his thighs and calves with meticulous care, circling his ankles and sweeping down to his feet. When she finished Ben reached down and lifted her to her feet.

"Now the back," he told her.

She wet the soap and worked the rich lather, again standing on tiptoe to reach his shoulders and massage the bubbles into the ropes of muscles. Her fingers danced down his spine, swept across his waist and over the tight cheeks of his ass. She paused uncertainly at the top of the cleft but Ben reached behind him, grabbed her wrists and pushed downward.

She dropped to her knees again and applied herself to the back of his legs with the same meticulous care she'd applied to the front of them. When she finished, she stood and would have placed the soap back in the inset holder but Ben stopped her with a single command.

"Now you can wash the crack of my ass. Take care with it, Grace. Pull the cheeks apart and get every inch of it."

His ass?

Fear and desire began their familiar battle inside her but desire was much, much stronger. Using the fingers of one hand, she separated the taut cheeks, her pussy clenching as her eyes traveled over the cleft from top to bottom, resting for long moments on the tight brown ring of his anus. Breathing heavily, she rubbed soap into every inch of the skin, running her fingertip over the dark opening, boldly scraping it with her fingernail.

Ben's whole body clenched when she did and she jerked her hand back.

"No." He tone was rough, uneven. "Don't pull away. Lather up your finger and push the soap inside."

Grace hesitated. Like so many other things she'd done with Ben, this was uncharted territory. She'd read about it once in one of her stories but never, ever done this.

Who would I have done it with anyway?

She and Joe had been so young and unsophisticated, barely learning their way around their sexual activity. And the thought of doing it with the few men she'd dated over the years disgusted her. Yet with Ben it beckoned like the most forbidden temptation.

She created as much lather on her fingers as she could, pulled the cheeks of his ass apart again and pressed the tip of one finger to the tight sphincter muscle.

"More," Ben commanded hoarsely. "Push, Grace."

Once past the opening her finger slid in easily, the dark tunnel tight and hot. Tiny spasms rocketed through her cunt and every pulse in her body vibrated.

"That's it, Grace. Fuck my asshole. Use two fingers. Do it."

She slid another finger in beside the first and moved them in and out in a steady rhythm. From her position on her knees she had a direct view of Ben's asshole and the movement of her fingers. She could also see the heavy sac with his testicles hanging below his buttocks. She couldn't believe how turned on she was getting. Impulsively she moved her other hand from his buttocks and reached between his thighs to cup and squeeze his balls.

Ben's breath whistled between his teeth. "Jesus, Grace." He jerked away from her. "Enough. You'll make me come."

And suddenly that seemed very important to her. "Please," she begged. "I want to do this for you."

He turned around and looked down at her, supplicant on her knees before him, the fine mist spraying down on her. The look in his eyes was indefinable but she wasn't afraid.

A muscle twitched in his cheek. Then his lips curved in a soft grin. "A good sub always wants to give her Master pleasure. Go for it, Grace. Finger-fuck my ass. Make me come in your hand."

Grace moved around on her knees, lathered both hands again, slipped two fingers of one into the now loosened muscles of his anus and gripped his cock with the other. Her hands moved in a coordinated rhythm, in and out of that hot dark tunnel, up and down on the thick shaft. She stared at his cock, totally absorbed in what she was doing, forcing herself to ignore the convulsive movements of her vaginal muscles demanding something to fill that needy channel.

It seemed to take only seconds before Ben's body tightened, tensed, his cock hardened even more in her hand and the thick semen began to spill over her hand. She moved her fingers in and out of his ass harder and faster, scraping the inner walls with her fingernails with each movement.

"Damn, damn, damn." Ben leaned forward, bracing his hands on the shower wall as his cock jerked and his hips thrust.

It seemed forever to Grace before the thick liquid stopped spurting and Ben's large body began to relax. Finally she released her hold on his shaft, slipped her fingers from his rectum and soaped and rinsed her hands.

Ben turned, lifted her until she was on her tiptoes and kissed her with the same intensity as when they'd first entered the suite. She was gasping when he finally released her.

"Just as soon as I get my breath back, darlin', I'm going to return the favor."

Grace trembled in anticipation, all the more so because she realized a hidden dark side of herself was unfolding and she was actually reveling in it.

* * * * *

Ben had soaped her all over, then had her stand with one foot on the built-in seat while he shaved off the fuzz that had grown on her cunt in the past few days. It was all she could do to control herself as his fingers pulled her labia this way and that and brushed against her sensitive clit.

Turning off the shower, he dried them both and carried her to the bed.

Rather than champagne—"We've done the fine vintage deal," Ben joked.—he ordered Lone Star beer from room service, the bottles arriving nestled in a large bucket of crushed ice. As soon as the waiter left he brought the beer into the bedroom and set it on the nightstand. Once again he cuffed her wrists to the bed, spread her legs wide and tied her ankles loosely. She squealed as Ben dribbled ice cold drops of the beer on her breasts and proceeded to lick them off.

"Like that, darlin'? I think you'll like what I'm gonna do next even better."

He held the bottle to her lips so she could drink, then set it on the nightstand. Reaching into the drawer, he brought out a slim leather case, about an inch and a half thick. He sat beside her on the bed as he opened the case and removed its contents.

"Bought this the other day. I've been dying to use it."

Her eyes widened as he held up a vibrator made of firm purple plastic, the rounded end ridged. She wasn't sure but she thought it was even bigger than Ben's magnificent cock.

Ben turned the control on the bottom and a low hum filled the air. A slow grin spread over his face.

"I want to drive you crazy with this," he said, his gaze hot. "Bring you to the edge again and again, until you scream for me to let you come." He leaned close to her. "Would you like that, Grace? For your orgasm to be totally under my control?"

That dark thrill slithered through her again and her pussy muscles flexed at the thought.

Ben traced the line of her slit with a fingertip. "Ah, my girl is getting wet at that thought. I think the role of the submissive suits you. We'll have to see just how far we can push this."

A tiny frisson of panic raced over her. Ben must have seen it in her eyes.

"Don't worry, Grace." He continued stroking her slit as he talked. "Just here, in these rooms. Just between us." He grinned. "But you never know what might turn you on. Get you hot. Arouse you. Shall I tell you a few things?"

"As long as you don't stop touching me," she gasped.

She wanted to shout at him to slide his fingers inside her, fuck her with them in his expert way but she knew the show was his. And *that* turned her on even more.

"I'm going to buy you some nipple rings, Grace, and put them on after I pull and tug on those luscious buds until they are ripe with color and aching to be used. Then I'm going to slip a tiny vibrator into that delicious cunt of yours. Do you know they make them with remote controls?"

"R-remote controls?" she stammered, trying to catch her breath as his fingertip circled her clit again and again.

"Uh-huh." He pinched her clit between thumb and forefinger.

Shafts of heat speared through her and moisture dripped from her cunt.

"Think about it, Grace," he went on, still pinching and rubbing her throbbing nub. "There we are, you and me, seated in one of these fancy restaurants on the Riverwalk, quiet music in the background, linen tablecloths, the works. The two of us with drinks in hand and I press the button on the remote in my pocket." He bent over her, his hand still busy between her legs. "Ever thought of having an orgasm while a restaurant full of people ate dinner around you?"

Hot and cold shivers raced over her body at the thought. What frightened her most was the idea she would actually do it. She was falling so deeply under Ben's erotic spell that she was reaching the point where anything he asked of her she'd do. All her carefully constructed walls were crumbling.

But in the next moment Ben clamped his mouth over one nipple and she forgot to be afraid about anything. He sucked on the hot bud and pulled it into his mouth, circling it with the tip of his tongue and lightly nipping at it with his teeth. Lazily he moved from one nipple to the other and repeated the treatment.

Grace arched up into his mouth, urging him to do more, lick more, bite more, whimpering in protest when Ben lifted his head.

"Remember how you liked the blindfold, darlin'?" he asked in his molten liquid voice.

"Y-Yes." He'd certainly been right about all her other senses being heightened.

"Then trust me when I say you'll enjoy this more with your eyes closed. When you can sink into darkness and do nothing but feel."

As he talked he'd shifted to open the drawer in the nightstand and pull out the silk scarf he'd used before. Folding it meticulously, he placed it across her eyes and tied it behind her head. Grace wanted to tell him to get to it, that she was hot and wanting and so wet she knew she was dripping.

She took a deep breath and let the darkness surround her. Felt Ben move into position between her thighs again, stroke his hand over her pussy, brushing the curls, tracing the line of her slit, rimming the opening of her vagina. Then she heard the faint hum of the vibrator and felt the rounded head of it as it teased her labia. Up and down. Up and down.

The low vibrations raced from the nerve endings in her cunt through her body, making her muscles tighten with need and her womb clench with desire.

"Feel good, darlin'?" Ben asked. "I'll bet it does. How does this feel?"

He began circling her clit with the tip of the vibrator and she jerked beneath its touch. She knew juices were pouring from her and the muscles in her pussy quivered, begging for something to fill that needy channel. She tried to shift her body, bending her knees and pushing up with her feet to urge Ben to plunge the thing inside her, but he had his own game plan. One hand pressed against her lower abdomen, keeping her in place, while the other continued the assault on her clit.

The orgasm began gathering inside her, pushing its way out and downward, tiny spasms already racing through her cunt.

And then he stopped. Pulled it away from her, although the humming continued.

"No, no, no." She twisted her head from side to side. "Don't stop. Not now."

"Shh, shh, shh," he soothed, reaching up to caress her cheek with one hand. "I don't want you to come yet. I want to see how high I can take you."

The tip of the vibrator was back, teasing at her clit again, following the path of her slit, then pressing the sensitive membrane between her cunt and her anus. He followed a pattern, not too long in any spot but paying equal attention to all of them.

Her body began to gather itself again, muscles preparing for the spasms that would grip them. There. She was almost there. She reached for it, strained for it.

And again the vibrator moved away.

She was sweating now, twisting helplessly on the bed, hands bound, eyes blindfolded, legs held wide by Ben's broad shoulders. She was totally at his mercy, an instrument for him to play as he chose.

And again, the excitement of it—no, the *craving*—that consumed her almost frightened her. Someone else was totally in control of her body and turning her into a wild animal and all she could think, when she could think at all, was *more, more, more.*

The open-mouthed kiss he placed on her cunt startled her and she jerked against her bonds then thrust her hips at him as much as she could.

Fuck me, she screamed in her head.

But Ben had his own battle plan.

To drive me crazy.

She bit her lip as the vibrator pressed against her skin again, now back and forth across her clit, now rimming the opening to her pussy. She was completely open to him, every part of her body his to tease and torment. And he was doing just that.

The vibrator moved away slightly, she sensed Ben moving, then something cool pressed against the tight ring of her anus.

"Gel," he whispered. "I want to be sure I don't hurt you, darlin'."

Grace tried to relax her buttocks as his palm cradled her and one finger slipped inside a little at a time. The moment he completely penetrated her he went to work with the dildo again, vibrating it again over her highly sensitized, swollen clit. She was panting with need now. He'd taken her up and brought her down so many times if she didn't come soon she was sure her body would implode.

"Please, Ben," she begged. "I need to come. Please, please, please."

"Tell me what you want, darlin'," he urged. "Say it for me."

"I-I-I want you to f-fuck me," she wailed. "Please."

"Tell me how," he insisted. "Say it, Grace."

Say it? She could barely form a coherent thought. She was so aroused, so close to the edge, it took all her willpower just to keep herself together.

"I-In my p-pussy." She thrust her hips at him. "With the vibrator."

"And where else?"

He was going to make her say it.

"In my ass."

As his finger worked its way in and out of her rectum the dildo slid into her vagina, pressing until the tip touched her womb. In an instant the vibrations increased

"Yesss," she screamed. "That's it. Oh god, that's it."

Her entire body was jerking and twitching, muscles convulsing, vaginal muscles clamping down on the dildo, her buttocks grasping hungrily at Ben's hardworking finger.

This time the climax would not be denied. Not all her willpower could have stopped it, no matter what Ben said. As if sensing he couldn't pull her back from the edge this time, he increased the tempo in both of her openings.

"Now, Grace," he commanded. "Come now. For me."

She exploded with such violence she was sure her body would fly apart. And just as she was at the top of her orgasm, Ben pulled both his finger and the dildo from her body, lifted her with both hands beneath her buttocks and plunged his condom-clad cock inside her to the hilt. Every sensation, every stimulation, was magnified because of the velvet blackness that she was floating in.

Her pussy muscles clamped down on his thick shaft, milking him as he rode her, thrusting in and out in a hard rhythm.

Grace had barely finished one orgasm before his movements hurled her into another. When his cock finally finished pulsing inside her wet channel, spilling his semen into the latex shield, every muscle in her body stretched like pulled taffy.

Ben's hot breath fanned her face as his lips brushed against hers in a gentle kiss. In the next moment, the blindfold was removed, the handcuffs unlocked and he was cradling her in his arms. His tongue licked the moisture from her skin, then he trailed featherlight kisses over her eyelids and her cheeks.

She wasn't sure whose heart she felt thundering against her ribs, hers or his, or who was working harder to drag air into oxygen-deprived lungs. It seemed they lay like that forever, bodies slick with sweat, heart working to settle down, a sated feeling enveloping them both.

Grace grumbled when Ben dragged her out of bed to the shower but he coaxed her in a soothing voice, pointing out how much better they'd sleep.

And he was right.

When they finally tumbled back into bed, she fell into a well of dreamlessness, limp as a noodle and satisfied beyond anything she'd ever imagined.

Chapter Eleven

🕉

Grace was sure she was having an out-of-body experience. Never in her life had she expected to be this uninhibited, this wild, this completely hedonistic. Saturday passed in an erotic haze. They slept late, ordered breakfast from room service, then took a long, leisurely erotic bath, washing each other with teasing strokes until Ben groaned in frustration, lifted her and, barely taking time to roll on a condom, drove up into her and fucked her until she didn't even know her own mind.

Ben dried her off and stretched her naked body on the bed and proceeded to lightly stroke every inch of her. Nerves she didn't even know she had came to life, snapping with need. He spent a long time paying homage to her breasts and nipples, sucking them into his mouth, nipping them with his teeth, soothing them with his tongue, plumping the breasts with his lean hands.

When she tried to pull him down to her, he cuffed her hands to the bed. Then he spread her legs wide, knelt between them and proceeded to lick every inch of her cunt, inside and out. His tongue stroked over her labia, twirled her throbbing clit then traced a wet line the length of her slit but it was barely a whisper of feeling. He was tantalizing her, driving her crazy, inciting a need in her that clawed to be satisfied. Even when he thrust his tongue inside her, the touch was almost like a feather, lightly stroking the walls of her cunt just enough to make them quiver and release a flood of her juices.

Kissing the inside of her thighs, he crawled up her body and began the process all over again. Kisses as light as a breeze. Tormenting kisses. Arousing kisses. And his erotic mouth, sucking, licking, biting until she was ready to scream.

"Please," she begged over and over.

"Please what, darlin'?" he asked in his warm molasses voice.

"Please…let me come."

"Let you come? Tell me what you really mean."

She was stretched on a rack of pleasure so taut she could hardly breathe, gasping out the words she knew he wanted to hear. "Please…fuck me. Fuck me," she screamed.

"With pleasure."

It took scants seconds for him to sheath himself. Grace watched him through slumberous eyes, the sight of his engorged, pulsing cock driving her arousal even higher.

"Hurry," she urged as he came over her.

"Not too fast," he teased, lifting her legs and placing them over his shoulders. His warm hands cupped her ass as he lifted her, positioned himself at her entrance and thrust himself home with one hard slide.

Grace sucked in her breath at the intrusion, her pussy muscles stretching to accommodate his girth. As big as he was, each time he penetrated her was like the first, her muscles straining to accept him, then clasping around him like a vise. Electricity shot through her, intensifying every sensation, burning through her with an all-consuming lust.

Ben stroked in and out of her with a steady rhythm. As open to him and exposed as she was, every inward thrust drove him to fill her completely. She heard soft moans filling the air, barely registering that they were hers. The heat inside her built and built until her skin felt too tight and her breath was trapped in her chest.

The spasms began low in her belly, rising from her womb and spreading outward through every muscle and fiber. They increased in their intensity as Ben drove harder and harder, his balls slapping against the cheeks of her ass, racing through her, pushing her higher and higher.

"Come now." Ben's voice was barely recognizable as he groaned through gritted teeth. "Now, Grace. Right now!"

She exploded around him as he pulsed inside her, the walls of her pussy grasping him and milking him. Every muscle convulsed over and over, shaking her, tossing her onto a newer, higher plain of pleasure. The spasms went on and on until Ben uttered one last groan, pulsed inside her one last time, lowered his legs and collapsed forward.

He braced his weight on his forearms, his rough breath fanning her face. Grace didn't think she'd ever catch her breath again. She for sure didn't want him leaving her body and whimpered when, with a huge effort, he pushed back and withdrew from the grip of her pussy. She tried to hold him in place by wrapping her legs around him but she was still trembling and had little strength.

"Be right back," he grinned down at her. "I'm not done with you yet."

In the afternoon they finally came up for air, strolled along the Riverwalk and ate dinner on a balcony overlooking the activity. Grace wore another of her new outfits, fussing again at Ben for his extravagance, but still and all, she felt as if she were living someone else's life. A life she planned to enjoy fully before she crashed back to earth.

Ben had turned off her cell phone and hidden it from her the night before, telling her Monday was soon enough to get back to business. It gave her an unexpected freedom, a sense of self that she suddenly realized was missing from her life.

She wanted to grab Sunday with both hands and hold on, turn back the clock, because once it was over she'd be back to the same old Grace Delaney. She wanted to live her fantasy as long as possible.

* * * * *

The air in the coliseum was even more charged when they arrived Sunday evening, an electricity that fairly crackled. This was the last night. The *big* night. The night when they'd learn who won the bucks, the buckles and the points to carry them to the Grand Nationals in Las Vegas.

Grace noticed that Ben was more tense than usual, although he tried to hide it from her. He was more meticulous checking his gear, more careful grooming Hotshot and soothing him. She watched him with hungry eyes, carefully storing up each and every memory.

She was sure a glow surrounded her after the nonstop sex they'd had earlier. Ben had come in her mouth, her cunt and then pulled her to her knees, spanked her ass until it was pleasantly warm before plunging hard inside her anus and taking her there. Finally he'd plumped pillows beneath her tummy, leaving her on her knees, and teased her from behind with the vibrator until she screamed for him to let her come. She wasn't sure she could stand one more shattering orgasm. She hadn't known what sex really was before this.

The finals of the calf roping event were called almost before she realized it. Ben mounted up and rode Hotshot into the chute. Danny once again found her a perch where she could see everything. When Ben held his hand up to show he had the calf roped and tied, the audience went crazy. It was obvious his time would be nearly impossible to beat.

When he rode out of the arena and dismounted, leading Hotshot to his stall, Grace started to hop down and join him but Danny shook his head at her.

"He'll want some time alone," the man told her. "The bull riding is the last event and he needs to gather himself."

So Grace stayed on her perch and tried to pretend that she was interested in the other events until they called for the bull riding. When it was Ben's turn, when he lowered himself onto the back of the charging monster, she had to force herself to watch, praying that he wouldn't get hurt. Watching the events close-up this way showed her exactly how much danger there really was.

He won the bull riding event going away, beating every other competitor in both time and form. But the crowd went crazy when he was announced as the all-around champion. He was driven to the center of the arena in the back of a pickup truck, waving to everyone. When the truck stopped in front of the stage he leaped out and climbed the stairs to the stage, where the chairman of the rodeo association presented him with his check and buckle. Then, following tradition, he rode around the arena once more in the truck, waving at everyone and grinning madly. When the truck stopped at the gateway to the hall, he jumped down and rushed to where Grace waited.

"The money's great but how about a kiss for the champ?" He yanked Grace down into his arms and kissed the breath out of her.

The cowboys and rodeo people standing around hooted, whistled and clapped, which only seemed to spur Ben on more.

"Just wait until I get you back to the room tonight," he whispered in her ear before letting her go.

And getting there seemed to take forever. Everyone wanted to shake his hand, offer congratulations, make plans to meet in Houston, the next stop on the tour. The Houston Stock Show and Rodeo would open in two weeks. Ben had already told her he wanted to trailer Hotshot there early and give the horse some playtime at the ranch a friend of his owned outside the city.

Then people insisted he join them at The Last Mile for at least one drink. He gave Grace a rueful look and murmured, "I'll make it up to you when we get back to the room, I swear it."

But she wanted him to enjoy his moment of glory. And she knew despite the excitement and backslapping, the uppermost thought in Ben's mind was how far the check would go toward helping him realize his dream.

They managed to leave The Last Mile after one drink, Ben hauling Grace out to the truck, then dragging her into the hotel when they got there. She had to hurry to keep up with his long stride.

"Someone would think you were in a big rush," she teased.

"Someone would be right," he muttered. "If there weren't people in this elevator with us I'd push the Stop button and fuck you right here."

He spoke in almost a whisper but the other couples looked at them with strange expressions. Grace was glad when they reached their floor. Just like the other night, Ben barely had the door closed and locked before he was pulling her clothes from her, throwing them wherever they landed, his own following. He cursed under his breath while he fumbled for the condom in his jeans pocket before tossing them aside, clumsy in his haste to roll it on. They were both so jacked up on adrenaline from the evening they were shaking.

Ben grabbed her thigh, lifting it and wrapping it around his waist. With a hard roll of his hips he drove into her, the head of his cock bumping the mouth of her womb. Her naked breasts were pressed hard into the wall of his chest, the fine mat of hair stimulating the sensitized surface of her skin. There was no foreplay, no preliminaries. This was pure, raw lust, sex with all the trimmings stripped away.

The moment she felt him inside her Grace climaxed, shuddering heavily in his grasp, her cunt muscles stroking the thickness of his shaft, pulling at him. As the aftershocks rolled through her Ben pressed his mouth to hers, forcing it open, plunging his tongue inside. With her mouth held captive he began his conquest of her pussy again, driving rapidly in and out, pushing her to yet another climax.

She convulsed in his grip, her arms wrapped around his next as his cock pulsed in the tightness of her vagina.

When he withdrew he let her leg down slowly and wrapped his arms around her, pulling her to his chest. His hands made soothing movements up and down her spine, his lips pressed against her hair and she could feel his heart galloping.

Her breath came in ragged gasps and her heart hammered against her ribs with thunderous force. If Ben hadn't been holding her she would have fallen to the floor in a heap.

Finally, letting out a ragged breath, he lifted her in his arms and carried her to the bed, stumbling so they both tumbled to the bed together. His mouth was gentle rather than ravenous as he trailed kisses down the column of her neck, into the hollow of her throat, across the slope of her breasts. Then he raised his eyes, searching hers, smoothing the hair back from her face.

"You okay, darlin'?"

"I think." Grace let out a shaky little laugh and looked up into his eyes. "Should I ask what that was?"

"You mean besides two people fucking against the door?" He let out another breath, as if trying to even the rhythm of his lungs. "I'd say it was an earthquake of seismic proportions." He cupped her cheek with one hand. "Fucking standing up is getting to be a habit, I think."

She felt the heat creep up her cheeks and Ben laughed.

"Don't tell me after everything we've done you're still embarrassed with me."

She buried her face against his shoulder. "I think the old Grace is still hovering near the surface. This is all so...so new to me, Ben."

"I know." He kissed her forehead. "That's what I love about you. Everything is new and fresh."

Love? Did he say the L word?

For a moment an unsettled feeling came over her and everything inside her body tried to go into defensive mode.

Then she told herself not to be foolish. It meant nothing. He was just paying her a compliment.

"You okay, darlin'?" he asked again, smoothing his hand over her shoulder and down her arm. "For a second there I felt you tense up on me." The teasing note left his voice. "I haven't pushed you too far, have I, Gracie?"

Yes but it was my choice. And I don't regret a thing.

"No." She shook her head. "Just trying to get closer to you."

His laugh was like thick honey. "I think we can handle that." He slapped her lightly on one cheek of her ass. "I think since I'm such a star tonight, I deserve to have my sub bathe me. What do you think? You did a fine job last time."

She lowered her lashes, the memory of that particular shower still vivid in her mind. "Your wish is my command, Master."

His laugh boomed again. "Excellent. Then let's get to it."

She scrambled out of bed and into the bathroom on legs still somewhat shaky, as much from expended energy as from anticipation. On the vanity counter she found a complimentary bottle of bath salts and dumped them into the bubbling water. Ben had to be sore, she reasoned, and any kind of bath salts would help ease the soreness in his muscles. Her nipples hardened and her cunt became slick as she thought of running her hands over every inch of his body. *Every* inch of it. The idea nearly stole her breath.

When the water had nearly reached the top she turned it off and pushed the button for the jets, setting the water to churning even more. She turned to call Ben, only to find him standing right behind her. He cradled her face in his hands and lowered his head, licking her lips with soft swipes of his tongue.

"You taste like the sweetest sugar," he murmured, his voice thick with expectation. "I'm going to tie you to the bed and lick and sip at every inch of you."

Grace shivered as delicious images rose in her mind. She lowered her eyes. "I read in a book that submissive are taught to call their Doms 'Master'. Is that right?"

His eyes darkened. "If we were doing this forever, it's something we could talk about. But for me it's not necessary. I only take what I need from the lifestyle. And we're just playing around the edges here. Okay?"

"Okay," she whispered.

If we were doing this forever?

That thought frightened her more than anything else.

She stepped into the tub and held her hand out to him. "Time for your bath."

"I know I'm going to enjoy this," he grinned, stepping into the roiling water.

He lowered himself until he was submerged up to his chin, closing his eyes as he let the water work its magic on him.

Jesus! How will I ever let her go after this? Better question, how could I keep her?

He and Grace came from two such different worlds. Adjusting to him and the things he'd demanded of her, sexually as well as emotionally, had been a big step for her. And for the first time in ages, he was getting true pleasure out of the sex.

She knelt between his legs and in a moment her small hands were rubbing bath gel into the tight muscles of his shoulders and his arms, fingertips to fingertips, working the stiffness out. Caressing his skin. His cock, spent thought it was, began to harden at the sensation.

As her hands moved over his chest, fingers trailing through the dark curls of hair, more feelings skittered over his body. And when she scraped a fingernail across first one nipple, then the other, he sucked in a breath. Her touch was electrifying, sending jolts of current straight to his misbehaving shaft.

Lower, lower her hands moved, bending his legs at the knees to wash from thigh to ankle, rubbing the gel into him with massaging movements.

Touch my cock, Grace! Touch it now!

He wanted to scream the commands but he gritted his teeth and bit the words back. He wanted this to be her show, although he wasn't sure how much teasing he could take. He chuckled silently to himself as the thought flashed though his mind that this was exactly what he did to her. Payback was hell!

"You need to turn around so I can do your back," she told him.

"Uh, Grace? I don't think you finished the front yet."

Her lips brushed against his in a featherlight caress. "I'm not finished yet. Right now it's back time."

He opened his eyes and turned himself so he was on his knees, bracing himself on the tub with both hands. He had to swallow the urge to grab her as her hands moved over his skin massaging in the gel. The water bubbling against him from the jets added to the soothing feel of her touch and he truly began to relax.

Except for his damn cock that wanted to stand up at attention and plunge itself into Grace's tight cunt.

When she rubbed the insides of his thighs he had to bite his lip to maintain his control. The worst was when her fingers brushed so very lightly across his sac, barely rubbing the gel into the skin. But then she cupped his balls and rolled them in her slender fingers, slid her gel-covered fingers up the length of his shaft from behind and he couldn't contain the groan that erupted from him.

Grace pressed against his back and nipped at his shoulder. "Like that, do you? I have something you'll like even better."

"You're a vixen, you know that?" He ground his teeth together.

"Fair is fair," she teased.

He was about to give her a smart remark when he felt her fingers at his anus, rubbing the gel into the tightened skin, then pushing through the opening and rubbing the tissues inside.

"Do you like that?" she whispered, sliding two fingers in and out.

"Like it?" he gasped. "I think I've created a monster."

"How about this?" she crooned and reached between his thighs to grip his cock with the other hand.

He nearly lost it when she began to stroke him up and down, her thumb caressing the flared head, fingernail gently probing the slit at the top. His first instinct was to stop her but he realized his body had moved past the point of controlling what was about to happen.

"Careful," he told her. "You're about to get more than you bargained for."

"Oh no." Her voice was sultry, hot with desire. "It's *exactly* what I wanted."

She moved her hand in bold strokes up and down his throbbing cock while delicate fingers probed his ass, scraping the nerves in that sensitive tunnel and sending shards of fire shooting through his body. His spine tingled and all his muscles tightened as his climax rose up in him. Then it burst on him, his cock pouring thick spurts of semen into Grace's hand under the water, his rectum clasping and clamping on her fingers.

"Grace!" he shouted as he rocked his hip and gave himself over to the sensations rolling through him.

It could have been one minute or a hundred before his body quieted and he fell forward on his crossed forearms, the water still churning around him. He felt Grace cleaning him with the bath gel, her touch soothing. When he could catch his breath he turned back around and startled her by grabbing her arms.

"You minx," he said, his voice thick. "I think you're learning too well."

She leaned forward and kissed him. "I remember how much you liked it in the shower. I just wanted to please you as you please me."

"You did, darlin'. Believe me, you did." He stood up, taking her with him. "But I think it's time to get out of here and get on with the rest of the evening."

She stood on the fluffy mat as he dried her off, then himself. She saw his hands shaking slightly and swallowed a tiny smile. Good, she'd gotten to him. If this was her last chance to immerse herself in the erotic, she was going full tilt, hoping Ben would wrap those memories around him when the tarted-up buckle bunnies gathered around him.

But not even she could have imagined how thoroughly wrung out she'd be when at last Ben drifted off to sleep. He had made good on his promise to tie her up and take his time licking every inch of her body. He'd added the vibrator for good measure, fucking her with it as he sucked her clit. Then he'd turned her over, positioned her on her knees and proceeded to fuck her ass until the orgasm that broke over her shook her to the very core.

At last, exhausted, the tumbled back on the mattress, Ben dragged the covers over them and kissed her temple.

"Sleep, darlin'. Pleasant dreams."

Chapter Twelve

ᔑ

Grace slept lightly, mostly dozing, her eyes on the readout of the bedside clock. She knew Ben wanted to make their goodbyes special in the morning but she wasn't sure she could handle it. These few days had been like a trip to another world for her. It had taken a lot of courage for her to shed her normal self and let Ben take the lead.

But saying goodbye was always messy. And the sooner she got back to her comfortable self, back to her normal routine, the better it would be. She could tuck these days away as a special erotic memory but even now she was beginning to wonder if she'd just flat out lost her mind.

Easing out of bed, she tiptoed to the other side of the room. Ben stirred as she slid from his embrace and made funny sleep noises but in seconds was out cold again. In all the mix of clothing she found the outfit she'd arrived in two nights ago—two nights? It felt like a month—and pulled it on. She found the little boot pin on yesterday's outfit and transferred it to the blouse she was wearing.

She was tempted at first to leave the clothes he'd bought for her. They really belonged to a Grace who didn't exist. But she knew Ben would be both angry and hurt, so she found the shopping bag and stuffed everything into it. She could hide these away with her memories.

Carrying the bag, her purse and her boots, she tiptoed out to the sitting room, eased open the door to the suite and slipped out into the hall. In the elevator she tugged on her boots, pulled a brush from her purse and ran it quickly through her hair. Looking at herself in the mirrored walls of the elevator car, she made a face at her image. Anyone looking at her could make a good guess at what she'd been doing.

Oh well. Too bad.

At the front door she asked the bellman to signal up a cab for her and in minutes she was speeding on her way home. Back to her safe house, her safe job and her safe life. The ball was over for Cinderella.

* * * * *

Ben rolled over, stretched his arm out and realized at once that something was missing. There was no desirable warm body in bed with him.

Forcing his eyes open, he saw the dent in the pillow where her head had been and smelled the lingering scent of her perfume on the sheets along with the musky aroma of sex. Bracing himself on one elbow, he scanned the room. Her clothes that had been tossed on the chair were gone. Not a good sign. And the bathroom door was open, so she wasn't in there. Also not good.

Maybe she was in the sitting room, waiting for him with hot coffee and rolls.

"Grace?" he called. "Darlin', are you out there lying in wait for me?"

When nothing but silence answered him he dragged his thoroughly tired body from the bed and padded naked into the sitting room. Nothing. No Grace. No anyone.

Shit!

He hadn't meant to sleep so soundly that she could slip away from him. It was something he'd been afraid of, the realization that she'd let herself out of her cage and the desperation to pull her walls in around herself again. A damn shame too. Grace was a vibrant, sensual woman just made for wild erotic sex. Not to mention the fact that he could talk to her about anything.

He shuffled back into the bedroom to check the clock. Ten o'clock showed on the LED readout. He had no idea how long she'd been gone. He needed to get his act together but his body felt as if a truck had rolled over it and his mind seemed to be missing a few parts.

He really didn't want to take time to shower but he needed the ice-cold spray to wake him up. Dressed hastily in jeans and the first shirt he could lay his hands on, he took the elevator down to the lobby and found the bellman at the stand out front.

"I don't know, sir," the man answered, when Ben asked him if he'd gotten a cab for a lone woman and described Grace to him. "I didn't come on until eight."

"Okay, where's the guy who was on duty before you?"

The bellman shrugged. "Probably home sleeping."

Ben tamped down his frustration, headed back to his suite, dug out his cell phone and punched in Grace's number at home. When the machine picked up he wanted to throw something.

"Hi. This is Grace Delaney. Leave a message, please."

"I'm not leaving any damn message," he shouted and disconnected.

Next he tried her cell but got voice mail. In disgust he threw the phone across the room and flopped back onto the bed. How had this ended up this way? Both of them knew it was what it was—a very pleasant interlude for both of them. Then he'd be moving on and she would pick up her life again. There were only two things wrong with the picture—he'd hoped she find herself more open to life after this and he wasn't at all sure he wanted to move on.

He'd wanted today with her. Planned on it. Maybe he could even have talked her into letting him spend a day in her house, see what she was like when she wasn't with him. Find out what made up Grace Delaney. He hadn't expected she'd steal away and leave him feeling so unsettled. Unfinished. Feelings that were foreign to him.

Well, what did he expect? He'd never given her any indication that they were having anything but a hot fling. It had been hard enough to coax her into that. He sensed right away she wasn't ready for something more than that and that was all he wanted. Right? No strings? Had a great time and goodbye? A young stud with an older woman?

Only he felt anything but young and his stud days were rapidly fading. Not to mention the fact that Grace really did put women half her age to shame. She was bright, funny, smart, sexy — hell, she was everything a man could want.

A smart man, that is.

Damn!

He'd love to get shit-faced drunk and feel sorry for himself but he had too many things to do. And a hangover wouldn't improve his already debilitated physical condition. Better to just check out, load up Hotshot and head for Houston before he hung around and got himself in trouble. If this was the way Grace wanted things, this was the way she could have them.

Only like repeatedly hitting a sore thumb with a hammer, he couldn't help himself from calling at least once an hour throughout the day in the pitiful hope that one time she'd pick up, answer the phone, tell him in person why she'd run.

* * * * *

Grace sat huddled on her couch in her favorite sweats, staring at the telephone. She'd indulged herself in a hot shower and a good cry when she got home that morning. She just wished she knew what she was crying about. The whole week seemed like something she'd dreamt. And wasn't that all it was supposed to be? Her own imagination giving life to the books she'd read, taking a leap to experience things for herself.

She'd known from the first day Ben would be leaving when the rodeo was over, moving on to the next show, the next event and finally to wherever he bought that ranch he dreamed about. But that was what had allowed her to break free. She could enjoy him for a short space of time, become another person. Then he'd be gone and she could pull in the boundaries of her life again. Anything more would be too much for her to handle.

The office didn't provide the distraction she needed, Reading financial projections and doing financial comparisons had suddenly lost their luster. But it was better than what she'd done that morning, moping around the house and listening to Ben rail at her on the answering machine. Unconsciously her hand lifted to the little boot that for some ungodly reason she'd pinned to her sweatshirt. As usual, it was warm to the touch, as if some mysterious energy radiated from it.

What was it the woman had said?

This pin has a long history of bringing lovers together... It will unlock the doors you hide behind.

Well, it had certainly opened those doors, no mistake about it. Just thinking about all the things she and Ben had done together made her face heat. It also made her nipples tingle and her pussy throb. She was sure if she touched herself she'd find a very damp crotch.

Well, good, Grace. After all these years you're turning into a slut.

No! her inner self shouted. *Not true!*

She had simply, led by the pin she was sure, managed to indulge herself in erotic fantasies she'd previously only read about. And the pin had brought them together as lovers, just not permanently. It wasn't supposed to. Was it?

You're being ridiculous, Grace. Get your act together. The party's over.

She was *glad* Ben was gone. Back here in her own environment she wasn't sure she could even look him in the face. The extent of her own eroticism frightened her, as well as the idea of a relationship with a man as sensual, as dominant as Ben Lowell. Especially one twelve years younger than she was. It was so foreign to her it made her stomach cramp. She needed her boundaries. They were safe.

That was it. She needed to be safe. In a safe life. Acting her age.

Then why did she feel as if a part of her life had been chopped away?

Burrowing into the pillows on the couch, she dozed off with her hand resting on the pin.

* * * * *

"Good morning, Grace."

Joyce Ritter's voice was perky as she greeted her boss but Grace saw a surprise in the woman's hazel eyes.

"Morning." Grace forced a smile. "You look as if you weren't expecting me."

"Well, you did say you didn't intend on coming in today…" Joyce's voice trailed off.

"Change of plans," Grace said in a tone that plainly said no questions.

"Good weekend? I can't remember the last time you took a day off. I thought we might be on a roll here."

So did Grace but she didn't plan to discuss it.

"It was fine, thank you." She took the messages Joyce handed to her as she breezed past the woman's desk. "Did you print out my calendar for today?"

"On your desk," Joyce called. "I, um, added Curt Sanderson at noon. He insisted he wanted to take you to lunch."

Grace's stomach sank. Another meal with Curt? The last one had gone so badly she wondered why he even bothered to call again.

He's safe, Grace. If you want a safe life, you need a safe man.

Swallowing back her refusal, she told Joyce, "Fine. Please call him and confirm. And tell him twelve thirty would be better." She was looking at her calendar. "My last two appointments this morning are liable to run late."

"I'm on it."

Dumping her briefcase, Grace popped a K-cup into the Keurig coffeemaker, pressed a button and in seconds held a steaming cup of hot liquid in her hands. She studied her calendar again as she sipped, mentally disciplining herself for the day ahead and her return to Grace Delaney mode. This was what she wanted, she told herself. Period.

Time to get on with life.

She had just finished with her ten o'clock client when Joyce buzzed to say her daughter was on the phone. Grace smiled as she picked up the receiver.

"Bridget? What a nice surprise. I thought you and Susan were still at Padre Island."

"No." Grace's twenty-one-year-old daughter laughed. "We came back yesterday. I took today off just so I could do laundry and get myself back in work mode. And see if you heard how Ryan's doing."

Both Bridget and her friend Susan worked for a law firm as paralegals. Bridget was still trying to decide if she wanted to stay with what she was doing or go on to law school. Her brother, twenty-year-old Ryan, was studying to be a geologist and was out in the Arizona desert on a work study program.

"I haven't talked to him in two weeks," Grace told her, "but he warned me then he'd be out of range for a while so I'm not worried."

175

"I can't imagine what he likes about being out there in all that sand and rocks. You dry up during the day and freeze your ass off at night."

Grace could almost see her daughter shudder and grinned to herself. "It's what turns him on, I guess."

"So," Bridget said with a sly tone, "I hear you spent the weekend with the hottest hunk in Texas."

Damn that Joyce and her big mouth. It had to be her. The Delaney offspring and Melanie Keyes weren't exactly on intimate gossip-sharing terms, despite the friendship the two women shared.

Grace cleared her throat. "I had a date. That's all."

"That's all?" Bridget's laughter pealed through the connection. "Mom, you haven't had a date in so long I didn't think you even knew how to spell the word."

"What about the Fiesta dinner?" she asked defensively. "And twice last month I went out with Jim LaGrange. Oh and dinner with Curt Sanderson."

Bridget laughed again, the sound warm and affectionate. "Those were business dinners. And fundraisers. They don't count. Anyway, I want to hear all about this tempting stud. I hear the date stretched out for more than one night."

Grace gritted her teeth. "He's just a man Melanie introduced me to. That's all. He was here for the rodeo."

"Oh." Grace could almost see the wheels churning in her daughter's brain. "Is he a sponsor? Or someone with the rodeo association?"

"No. He isn't."

"He isn't?" Silence, then Bridget squealed. "Ohmigod, he's a *competitor!* Mom, you had a date with a *cowboy!* Ohmigod, I want to hear all about it. Can we have lunch?"

No way was she going to put herself in position for her sharp daughter to cross-examine her. She'd give too much away.

"I'm having lunch with a client," she said. "And then I've got a really busy week."

"You're avoiding me. This must be some cowboy."

"Whatever he is, he's gone now, so there's nothing to talk about."

"Gone?" Bridget's surprise was obvious. "Gone where?"

"To the next rodeo, my darling daughter. End of discussion. Time to hang up."

"You can't hide from me forever," Bridget told her. "I'll get you when you least expect it."

That's what Grace was afraid of. "Listen, Bridget…"

"Oops. Gotta go. My cell phone's ringing. I'll catch you this week."

Grace hung up feeling decidedly unsettled. Maybe it was a good thing after all that she was having lunch with Curt. He was just what she needed to get this entire past week out of her head.

* * * * *

"You are certainly one surly son of a bitch," Clay Morgan said to his friend.

They were sitting on the front porch of the ranch house with second cups of morning coffee. Clay had been a champion bronc buster until a broken leg finished him. He'd taken his substantial winnings and bought this cattle ranch outside Houston and seemed to be running a successful operation. It was what had given Ben the idea for himself.

Ben had been at the ranch for a week, resting Hotshot and putting himself back together. During that time Clay had been doing his damndest to engage Ben in some kind of conversation without any results. He was having the same dismal luck this morning.

Usually when Ben visited the two men spent afternoons riding out to check the herd, riding fences with the hands, or just sitting on the porch talking about life and the good old days. Evenings they'd find a good steak house or Mexican restaurant, take their time over food, then hit a bar and size up the women.

But this time Ben had kept pretty much to himself, refusing all of Clay's offers of entertainment or activity, instead just sitting on the fence rail watching his horse romp and play or riding out by himself to find a place away from everyone. Most questions had received a one-word answer.

Ben knew Clay was right. He *was* surly. But he couldn't seem to shake himself out of it.

"Gotta be a woman," Clay mused. "Yup. Nothing but a woman turns a man into a grizzly bear."

"You think you could just shut up for a while?" Ben snapped.

"Oho!" Clay grinned. "I'm right. And it must be one hell of a woman to put you in this kind of a mood. What did she do, turn you down?"

"No, she didn't. And I said shut up."

Ben could feel Clay's eyes on him, studying him.

"So she didn't turn you down," the man said finally. "That's not the problem, is it? You did your usual walkaway and now you can't seem to let this one go. Try to tell me I'm wrong."

Ben said nothing, just worked on his coffee.

Clay snapped his fingers. "Got it. She left you *before* you could run off and you're pissed." He leaned over to look at Ben. "Or maybe it's a lot more than that. Don't tell me you actually fell for some broad."

Ben glared at his friend and stood up.

"You better do something about this, buddy boy," Clay called after him. "You've got to compete this week and you can't do it unless your head's on straight. Either go and get her or wipe her out of your mind."

Ben's answer was to slam the door behind him as he walked into the house.

But that afternoon he drove into Houston by himself and spent a fair amount of time shopping for some very particular things. He spent a long time searching for exactly what he had in mind. When he finally located what he wanted, he had them gift-wrapped, then took them to a UPS store and had them packaged and shipped, with a short note tucked inside.

Now it was out of his control and Clay was right. He needed to concentrate on the upcoming rodeo.

* * * * *

What the hell am I doing here? I must be losing my mind.

All week long Grace had been closing doors again, shutting herself up in her nice, neat, well-ordered existence. She ignored Joyce's remarks about her suddenly snippy personality and deftly avoided her daughter. Shuffling numbers and financial projections, reading spreadsheets, preparing financial statements all had her marching to the same old tune. *Good,* she told herself. *This is who I am.*

Two lunch dates with Curt Sanderson had turned into a third, for dinner. Tonight when he'd driven her home she'd taken a deep breath, deliberately pushed Ben Lowell out of her mind and invited Curt to come in. There was no mistaking the gleam in his eye, not then and not now. He'd been after her for a long, long time and he could see the door to paradise cracking open for him.

At least paradise as he saw it.

Grace looked at him now lounging on her couch, holding a glass of wine. He'd removed his jacket and tie, tossing them over the arm of a chair and opening the top two buttons on his dress shirt. Grace noted the exposed skin was smooth and wondered if he was one of those men with a hairless chest. A picture of Ben's chest flashed into her brain, with its thick dark curls layered over rock-hard abs.

Stop it!

But instead of Ben, her "young stud", she was facing a man several years older than she was and, she was sure, on the down side of his sex drive.

Sex isn't everything!

Really?

No but it would do until something better came along.

Stop it! she told herself again.

Grace took a healthy swallow of her wine, deliberately banishing the teasing images from her mind. *This* was what she wanted. *This* was what her life should be. Sedate. Mature. *Safe.*

"You know," he said, leaning forward, wineglass held loosely in one hand, "I've always thought you and I would make a good couple, Grace."

Her stomach knotted and tension raced through her body.

Here it comes.

"Oh?" she tried to make her voice casual. "What do you mean? In what way?"

"We're both mature people, not looking for adventure in life. Right?"

Speak for yourself.

"I suppose," she said, noncommittal.

"I know you're aware that I have a tremendously stable financial situation. A beautiful home that would be graced by your presence. We could travel, do a number of things together." He leaned even closer. "I could take care of you, Grace. You wouldn't have to work anymore. You could be a lady of leisure after working yourself nearly to death all these years."

"But I love my work," she protested. Doing nothing all day held no appeal for her.

"You say that now," he countered, "but when I show you how relaxing life could be, you'll wonder why you waited so long."

"Curt, I still have a son in college who's my financial responsibility..."

"And it would be my greatest pleasure to help you with that."

She drank the rest of her wine in two swallows, hoping it would relax her. "Let's think about it. For a while, anyway."

"All right. You know," he pointed out, "this is the first time I've been in your home. A pleasant surprise. How about giving me the tour?"

Okay, she thought, here it comes. He wasn't shifting gears, just trying another tack. A subtle nudge toward her bedroom so he could make his move. And what would she do when she got there?

Suck it up, Grace. Forget adventure. This is what you want, right? How bad can it be?

As she led him through each room, he maneuvered himself closer and closer to her, until by the time he reached her bedroom his arm was around her, almost but not quite casually. When he pressed his hand against her back she let herself be turned toward him, knowing what was coming.

She steeled herself for the kiss, vowing not to compare it with Ben's. Surprisingly it wasn't as bad as she expected. His lips were dry and firm and when he pressed his tongue against the seam of her lips and slipped it inside, it didn't offend her as she'd expected. Not in Ben's class, by any means but acceptable, at least.

Stop it. Forget Ben.

"You don't know how long I've wanted to do this," he told her when he lifted his head, then bent to her mouth again.

His hands were gentle on her back as they stroked up and down her spine. With her body pressed against his she could feel the thickness of his erection and wondered if he'd taken something in preparation for his expected big night. Certainly Ben never needed anything. He was always ready. Hard and thick.

Once again she pushed thoughts of Ben from her mind. They weren't part of her plan to settle herself into the lifestyle she knew was best for her. Especially at her age. Had Ben ever realized how much more the age difference would matter as they grew older? That when she was in her sixties he'd still be barely past fifty?

Curt kissed her cheeks, her nose and then her lips.

"Grace, I wanted you from the moment I saw you. Such a vibrant woman, I thought. Someone who could brighten my life." He let out a shaky breath. "I was beginning to think it was never going to happen." He raised his head slightly to look at her. "People our age don't usually find a second chance, you know. And you've been widowed far longer than I have. I thought maybe you didn't plan to let another man into your life."

People our age? Is he kidding? I haven't even started living yet.

The thought kicked her in the stomach. She *hadn't* started living, at least not until Ben. And she'd run away from that as fast as she could, frightened as the walls of her carefully constructed existence began to shatter and crumble.

"Grace?"

He obviously was waiting for some kind of response from her.

"I don't know *what* plan you're talking about, Curt," she said lamely. "I've focused on the children and the business for so long…"

"It's all right." His kissed her cheek again. "I'll give you plenty of time to get used to me." He rested his forehead on hers, his hands wandering up and down her spine.

"May I spend the night here with you? You don't know how much I want to. I don't think I want the evening to end just yet."

Her stomach muscles knotted, the thought of sex with Curt making bile rise suddenly in her throat. "Um, Curt, that's probably not such a good idea. My daughter sometimes pops in early in the morning before she goes to work."

"It's Friday night," he pointed out. "I don't think she works on Saturday."

"That makes it even more likely she'll stop by." She patted his cheek. "This has been wonderful, Curt. But it's been a full week for me. I could use a good night's sleep."

"So you're saying you want me to leave," he said in a flat tone.

"Don't be upset." She patted his cheek again. "There'll be other nights."

Like hell.

"All right," he sighed. "Never let it be said I'm not a gentleman."

Grace walked Curt to the door.

He took both her hands in his, kissing the backs of them. "When can I see you again?" His eagerness was obvious. "I want you to think about all the things I said earlier. Maybe we can discuss them again over dinner in the next day or two."

"Let's see how my week goes," she waffled. She'd have to find a way to tell him this just wasn't going to work.

Easing him onto the porch, she let him pull her into his arms one more time, determined to at least end the evening with as much grace as possible. The crash landing would come soon enough and it wasn't his fault that he wasn't anywhere near what she wanted. She accepted another kiss from him, murmured something indistinguishable and shooed him to his car.

Scratch one client, she thought ruefully, waving as he drove away. *When he finds out I have no intention of letting him into my life, he's sure to take his business someplace else.*

Tonight had certainly been one of the least successful events in her life. Why in hell had she thought this was what she wanted? Better yet, why had she thought going out with Curt would erase the memories of herself with Ben—memories so wanton she blushed when she remembered them. This was not working at all and she was about to lose a very good client because of it.

Maybe just giving up men and sex was the best idea. It didn't seem to be working out this way at all. Rather than feeling settled, stable, she went to bed with her body unsatisfied and dreamed of a cowboy with an enormous erection walking toward her and grinning.

* * * * *

As if the fates were determined not to make a liar out of her, Grace opened her door Saturday morning to find a grinning Bridget on her porch.

"I come bearing gifts." She lifted a white box tied with string. "Chocolate croissants from your favorite bakery. How about some mocha cappuccino to go with it?"

Grace sighed and shoved her fingers through her tousled hair. "You don't think we'll die of a chocolate overdose?"

Bridget laughed. "One of the best ways to go."

"Okay." Grace stepped back to let her daughter in. "How about starting the coffee while I brush my teeth and wash my face."

"Good deal," she said, heading for the kitchen.

Grace sighed again and trudged to her bedroom. In the adjoining bath she did her best to make her hair and face presentable, then dragged on a pair of jeans and a blouse. She knew Bridget was here with a plan of attack and she felt somehow defenseless in her robe.

Everything was on the table when she entered the kitchen and sat down.

"We don't do this enough," Bridget told her as she poured the coffee.

"You're busy," Grace pointed out, "and so am I. But you're right. We need to make more time for each other."

They'd been close ever since Bridget was a young child and they still spoke several times a week on the phone but they were each busy with their own lives.

"So," Bridget said, picking up a croissant and breaking off a piece. "I hear you've been seeing Curt Sanderson."

Grace grimaced. "Like I said the other day, Joyce has a big mouth."

"Mom, it's not like she called me and blabbed or anything. I was looking for you a couple of times and she said the two of you were having lunch. Oh and she thought you had dinner plans last night."

"Which is nobody's business but mine."

"So how was it with the old goat?" Bridget popped the piece of roll in her mouth and watched her mother with bright eyes.

"He's not an old goat. Be respectful." Grace took a swallow of coffee, hoping the hot liquid would wake up her brain cells. Her sleep had been restless and she had the feeling she wasn't hitting on all cylinders.

"Are you kidding me? He's definitely in the elderly category and looks like someone created him out of Play-Doh that's now drooping."

Grace burst out laughing, because the description was so appropriate. That's exactly what she'd felt last night when she'd forced herself to go out to dinner with him so she could establish a nice "safe" relationship and get Ben Lowell out of her mind.

"You're unkind," she said but she couldn't hide her grin.

"He's not what you want, Mom." Bridget chewed thoughtfully on another piece of croissant, her eyes glued to Grace's face.

"Oh and I suppose you know what's good for me?"

"I know that Joyce said a hunky cowboy put a smile on your face and made you glow. I know I tried a bunch of times to reach you and couldn't so I figured out exactly where you were. So what happened to him?" An impish grin turned up her lips. "He sounds like someone too luscious to lose."

"He's gone," Grace said in a flat voice. "He was only here for the rodeo."

"And you spent all that time with him?" Bridget squealed. "Ooh, I'm jealous."

"He's probably more suited to you than me, anyway." Grace fiddled with the roll on her plate.

"What's that supposed to mean?" Bridget's eyes widened and she grinned again. "Oh, I get it. He's younger than you."

"That's part of it," Grace agreed.

"Damn! Mom, the older woman-younger man thing is very 'in' right now, didn't you know? Besides, you look ten years younger than you are."

"That's not the point."

"That *is* the point," Bridget argued. "He could probably have his pick of tons of women and he chose *you*. Doesn't that tell you something?"

"But—"

"But nothing." Bridget said. "You so need someone like him and not like Curt Sanderson." She wiped chocolate from her hands and leaned across the table. "You think I don't know you've buried yourself since Dad died, taking care of Ryan and me and building a successful business? You made yourself old before your time. Dad died before I could ever get to know him but I'll bet he'd hate what you've done to yourself."

Grace's whole body clenched at the mention of Joe's name. She pushed the plate with her croissant away from her and turned to stare out the big kitchen window.

"How can you even know what your father would want?" she asked. "You were barely a toddler when he died."

"Because I've seen the pictures of the two of you." Bridget was relentless now. "You both looked so alive, so...so...full of joy and happiness and pleasure." She reached across the table to touch her mother's hand. "My favorite picture is the one of him in a t-shirt and jeans in an old lounge chair and you in shorts and a blouse sitting on his lap. Every time I saw that picture I thought, that's what I want when I get married. And when I got older, I added, and I bet they had a great sex life."

"Holy hell, Bridget." Grace pulled her hand away as heat crept up her face. "That isn't something you should be discussing with me."

"Why not?" Bridget cried. "I want someone who can put a glow on my face the way Dad did for you." She leaned back in her chair. "And you won't get it from Curt Sanderson, believe me."

"Well." Grace pushed back from the table. "It's immaterial because love has nothing to do with this. He's not interested in it and neither am I."

"Then ride it for as long as it lasts," Bridget insisted. "Don't miss out on what's out there for you, Mom."

After Bridget left, still lecturing as Grace shoved her out the door, Grace poured herself a fresh cup of coffee and sat in the big armchair in the living room, staring at the family pictures displayed everywhere and letting her mind wander. The mention of Joe's name had been like a sharp knife, stabbing at her. He had once told her if anything happened to him, he wanted her to continue to embrace life, not hide herself away. She'd brushed it off, not having the least idea that his death was much closer than either of them expected.

Overwhelmed by grief, she'd pulled the frayed edges of her life together as best she could, determined to be both mother and father to her two children. Provide a good home for them. Give them security.

Safety.

In doing so she'd sublimated all her needs as a woman, to the point where she hadn't been sure any part of her had survived. Bridget was right. She and Joe had had a great sex life, despite the fact they were both young and inexperienced. Would they have evolved into the kind of things she did with Ben? Maybe, but she'd never know. Instead she'd buried her sexuality until she hadn't been sure it even existed anymore.

When she began reading erotic romance novels, she allowed herself to fantasize, to daydream about experiencing erotic adventures, never realizing or expecting she'd have the opportunity. Or the courage to explore her own hidden desires.

She couldn't decide if she was more frightened by the extent of her response to the books or the sudden knowledge that she could experience pleasure beyond anything she imagined. Walking into the powder room, she examined her face in the mirror over the sink. What did the world see when they looked at her? A respectable woman who didn't have much fun in life? Or someone hiding from what life had to offer?

Grace shook herself. This was doing her no good. And despite what Bridget said, her interlude with Ben had been just that. She couldn't imagine any way she could fit him into her life. And she was sure she wouldn't fit into his.

Chapter Thirteen

Ben leaned back in his chair and tilted his beer bottle to his lips. All around him in the bar, riders from tonight's events at the Houston Stock Show and Rodeo were backslapping winners, commiserating with losers, soaking up Smoky Joe's beer as fast as the bar owner could serve it and making none-too-subtle passes at the willing buckle bunnies. Ben had been adding his fair share to the noise, something new for him since he usually kept to himself. And even when he hooked up with a girl, he did it quietly and discreetly. His business was his business.

But tonight he'd been pouring down the beer, pinching ass, splitting the air with piercing wolf whistles. At the moment a blonde with tousled curls and breasts that could knock your eyes out was standing between his chair and Lonnie Clark's, purring over both of them.

For a moment an image of Grace flashed across his brain before he deliberately forced it away. Like everyone else in the bar he was still fueled with adrenaline from the night's events. The rodeo had two more days to run and again he was the leading contender in his events. He should be celebrating instead of turning into a maudlin drunk.

He grabbed the blonde and hauled her into his lap, letting the edge of his fingers graze the side of a breast as he curled his arm around her. Instead of jerking away, she pressed herself closer to him.

"Buy me a drink, cowboy?" Her voice had the husky quality of someone who'd had one too many whiskeys in their life.

"Maybe more than one, if you promise to be good to me." He nuzzled her neck and let his hand rest more firmly on her breast.

She leaned over to whisper in his ear. "I can be very, very good."

"Well, all right, darlin'. What are you drinking?"

Three beers later, hoping he didn't kill both of them on the drive back to the hotel, he packed her into his truck and took off. They made as sedate a trip through the lobby as they could, considering the blonde's fit of giggles. The moment he shut the door to his suite he pulled her into his arms and took her mouth in a predatory kiss. His tongue speared into her wetness as she opened for him and he dueled with hers, exploring, stabbing, sucking. His hands moved up to cup her breasts, pinching her nipples through the thin fabric of her blouse and he ground his erection against her mound.

"Strip," he gasped as he lifted his head.

Something flickered in her eyes at the crude command but she found a smile somewhere and began to undress. Ben was out of his own clothing in seconds, toeing off his boots and yanking his boxers and jeans down with one push of his hands and ripping his t-shirt over his head.

"Come here," he said, lifting the blonde and carrying her to the bedroom.

Impatiently he jerked back the covers on the bed, dropped her on it and followed her down. His hands gripped her thighs, spreading them apart before he settled himself between them and ran his tongue the length of her slit.

"Ooh," she squealed. "I love that. Do me, cowboy."

Suddenly a warning bell went off in the back of his alcohol-soaked brain. He looked at the woman in his bed, her body suddenly fuzzy as his eyes lost focus, and he collapsed beside her.

He felt her push his shoulder.

"Hey, cowboy, you awake? Come on. I'm hot and ready for you."

"Jus' a minute," he slurred, but his eyes slammed shut with no effort from him and a thick blackness wrapped itself around him.

He awoke in the early hours of the morning, restless, vaguely disturbed about something that he couldn't quite define. The sight of the naked woman next to him in bed shocked the cobwebs out of his brain. He knew nothing had happened because he still had all his clothes on. Even his boots, and he knew he'd never fucked a woman with his boots on. He slipped out of bed, grabbed clean clothes and headed for the shower. But all the hot water in the world couldn't wash away the slimy feeling that captured him when he realized what he'd almost done.

Finally, clean and dressed, he called room service and ordered coffee. Then he bent over the nude woman and shook her awake as gently as he could.

"Hey. Rise and shine. Time to go home." He backed away from the bed. "I ordered coffee. You should get dressed before the room service waiter gets here."

"Can I tell you what a loser you are?" she asked, rubbing her eyes.

"Yeah, yeah, you're absolutely right. But you still need to get dressed."

She started to say something else but instead gathered her clothes from the other room and carried them into the bathroom. By the time the coffee arrived the blonde had joined him in the sitting room, looking as put together as was possible at that hour of the morning.

"Have some coffee before you go." He nodded at the tray. "Did you leave a car at Smoky Joe's?"

She shook her head. "I came with a girlfriend."

He found his wallet and handed her three twenties. "Cab fare. I don't know how far away you live."

She took the money silently, stuffed it in her jeans pocket and poured herself a cup of coffee. Neither of them said a word while they drank the hot liquid. Finally she put down her empty cup.

"Let me just say you're the first man who ever fell asleep before. I guess your reputation is better than your actions. Don't bother looking for me next time you pass through here." She found her purse where she'd dropped it on a table, then turned back to him. "You know, you didn't even ask my name."

Ben felt a flush of shame but he couldn't figure out what to say at this point to make the situation better. He couldn't shake the feeling he'd done something wrong.

"It's Tina."

He raised his eyes to look at her. "What?"

"My name. It's Tina."

"Oh. Well, Tina, thanks. You're a great gal."

"Yeah, right." She opened the door but before stepping into the corridor she turned back one last time. "And by the way, you're an asshole."

She slammed the door as hard as she could and was gone.

Ben sank into the nearest chair, dropping his head into his hands. He'd thought another woman would wipe away Grace's invisible prints on him but that was a true fucking disaster. Except of course there hadn't been any fucking, for which he was grateful. Somehow he would have seen it as soiling what he and Grace had done together. Would Grace Delaney haunt him forever?

Shit!

He wondered if she'd gotten his package yet and if so, what her reaction had been.

* * * * *

192

"I guess we can scratch one client," Joyce commented, walking into Grace's office as Curt Sanderson stormed through the outer door. "Man, what did you do? Tell him his taxes are going up?"

"Worse than that." Grace unclipped her hair, ran her fingers through it then pulled it back into the clip again. The early morning headache was now a real headbanger. She'd have given anything not to have gone through the scene with Curt.

"Wait, let me guess." Joyce closed the door, poured Grace a cup of coffee from the carafe on the credenza and carried it to the desk. "You told him you weren't going to see him anymore."

Grace nodded, rubbing her temples in an effort to ease the tension gripping her head.

"Well." Joyce sat on the corner of the desk and handed the coffee to Grace. "I know I'm just the secretary—"

"Oh can it," Grace snapped. "We've worked together for fifteen years. You know me almost better than my kids do."

"All right then. I didn't think you should have gone out with him to begin with."

"Because he's a client."

"That has nothing to do with it. Honey, he is way too old and stodgy for you."

"He's sedate," Grace protested. "And settled."

Joyce snorted. "He's settled all right. He may be only in his early sixties but he could pass for seventy any day."

"Maybe running an engineering firm took too much out of him," Grace offered, drinking gratefully from her cup.

"Bullshit. That man was born old. Have you looked at yourself in the mirror, Grace? You could give women ten years younger than you a run for their money." She leaned closer. "Besides, you have something most of those idiots don't have."

"And I know what it is—wrinkles and falling gravity."

"I am going to smack you." Joyce stood up and paced in front of the desk, then stopped, hands on hips. "You listen to me. You're smart, funny, educated and as sexy as all hell. Don't you dare downplay yourself."

Sexy? Me? Not even Joe ever called me sexy.

"Are you listening to me?" Joyce demanded.

Grace looked up at her. "Yes, Mother, I am."

"Mother, ha! Your mother wouldn't give you this advice. Go track down that cowboy who put such a glow in your face and tie him to the bed."

"Joyce!" Grace's face heated. "For god's sake."

Joyce put both hands on the desk and leaned forward until she was eye to eye with her boss. "And do it pretty damn soon. Life goes by too fast." She stood up. "Enjoy your sexuality, Grace. Don't run away from it."

"Easier said than done," Grace muttered.

Breaking habits of a lifetime took more courage than she was sure she had. A week was one thing but more than that? She shivered with both anticipation and fear of loss of control. That was it, the sticking point. Opening herself up sexually and emotionally to someone like Ben let all her desires out of the closet where she'd hidden him. The control she'd maintained for more than twenty years was in danger of shattering and she didn't know if she could survive.

"Grace?" Joyce's voice seemed to come from far away. "Honey, are you all right?"

Grace shook herself. "I'm fine." She forced a smile. "Thanks for the pep talk. I guess we'd better get Curt's files together and send them to him."

Joyce gave her a wicked grin. "Not so fast, as they say on television. I may be able to hang onto the old goat, once his hurt pride simmers down."

"Well, if you think you can, go ahead. But be sure not to call him an old goat to his face."

Joyce laughed softly as she closed the door.

Grace's fingers stole to the little boot pin nestled on her collar. She hadn't been without it, even pinning it to her robe, as if the wisdom she needed to make the right decision would radiate from the exquisite little piece of jewelry.

And what if she tracked Ben down and he decided he didn't want her anymore? Could she handle that?

Sighing, she opened a file on her computer and began to study a spreadsheet. Rows of numbers ought to settle her down.

* * * * *

Ben was shocked when he opened the door to his suite to find Clay Morgan standing there. His friend had said very little, just taken him by the arm, led him out to his truck and hauled his ass to the ranch. First thing when they arrived Clay had his housekeeper put together a solid breakfast for the two of them, refusing to discuss anything until the food was gone.

Ben hardly felt like eating but he knew with all the beer in his system he needed food to absorb it so he obediently cleared his plate. But when he finished and the housekeeper had refilled his coffee cup, he leaned back in his chair and eyed his friend.

"Okay, let's have it. Who tattled on me?"

Clay stared right back at him. "I wouldn't call it tattling, exactly."

"Oh? What, then?"

"Concern." Clay set his cup down. "People are concerned about you. It's obvious you've got a bug up your ass about something and too many people are afraid you'll kill yourself riding the bulls if you don't get your act together."

195

"If that's all it is, you can stop worrying. I'll ride as well as I always have." Ben knew his tone was belligerent but he didn't need people sticking their nose in his business. Especially since he was trying to figure out just what that business was.

"Sunday night's a big night for you," Clay pointed out. "It might be your last if you can't focus and one of those big mothers stomps you to death."

"I'm fine," Ben insisted, swallowing the rest of his coffee.

Clay was silent for a moment, studying his friend. "Why don't you call her? This stewing over it isn't doing you any good."

"Leave it alone," Ben growled. He couldn't tell Clay he'd made his move and now it was up to Grace.

"Ben, we've been friends for a long time." Clay leaned forward, elbows on the table. "I never thought I'd see you this twisted up over a woman. She must be something."

Ben shifted his gaze to stare out the big window. "She's everything and I treated her like it was nothing. Footloose and free, you know me."

Clay made a rude noise. "So quit sucking your thumb and do something about it."

Ben just shook his head. "We'll see. She's...different." His eyes glazed as images of Grace in sexual abandon flashed across his memory. "She locked herself up in a box for most of her life and I think finding out who she really is scared the pants off her."

"Then you've got your work cut out for you. Meanwhile, I'm keeping you out of trouble until tomorrow night. You won't be much good to anyone if you wreck yourself because you're too drunk or too distracted. And tomorrow night is important if you still plan to go to Vegas." He pushed his chair back from the table. "Come on. Let's take a ride to the south pasture and check on the new calves."

* * * * *

"I told Joyce I'd hand this to you." Melanie Keyes breezed into Grace's office without knocking, a small padded brown envelope in one hand. She waved it at Grace. "UPS just delivered it. The cowboy's sending you presents?"

Grace wasn't sure if she was shocked or embarrassed. She stretched out a hand but Melanie pulled hers back. "Uh-uh-uh. Not until you answer some questions first."

Grace sighed. "Come on, Mel. I'm in no mood to play games. I've had a bitch of a day and I want to go home and slide into a bubble bath. Give it here."

Melanie flounced to the couch, far enough away that Grace couldn't reach her without getting up and walking over. "You haven't returned my calls, or even sent me an email saying you're dead or something. I heard from at least six people that you were dating that disgusting idiot Curt Sanderson. I want to know what's going on." She crossed her legs. "After all, if it weren't for me you wouldn't have met Ben Lowell in the first place."

"I'm not sure if that was a blessing or a curse."

"It can't have been too much of a curse," Melanie pointed out. "Ross said the two of you were glued together for most of the week."

"Oh?" Grace arched her eyebrows. "And just how would Ross know?"

"Well, for one thing, he saw you there with Ben several times and the two of you sure didn't look like you were making war. He said Ben's never been with any woman more than two nights. Ever."

A tiny thrill skittered along Grace's spine. Was that true? Had she really been the exception to his practice? But he made it plain from the beginning this was just a temporary thing. In his head he was already buying that ranch in Wyoming and he'd never once indicated she might have a place there.

197

And hadn't she been just as happy? Ben was an aberration, a step away from her safe, secure existence, where erotic love existed only in her dreams and the novels she read and the rest of her life fit neatly into its design. So Curt Sanderson had been a disaster. So what? There had to be other men out there, men older than she was, who could provide a stable, proper existence, men who wouldn't turn her off in bed. She was forty-four, for god's sake. What would she do with a man twelve years younger, a man into BDSM but who made her body sing and her blood race? Who made her laugh? Made her want more? Her hand stole to the pin on her collar and warm flooded her.

Stop it.

"I can hear your brain frying," Melanie said, bouncing the little package in her hands. "Aren't you even curious about what's in here? I am."

Grace shook herself mentally. "Ben Lowell was...interesting," she said. "It was a great week but now we each have lives to go back to."

"You call this a life?" Melanie swept her hand around the office. "If it weren't for your business you'd have *no* life. You hardly date and haven't for years. You've buried yourself in work and your kids. When do you get to do something for yourself?"

"Honest to god." Grace threw up her hands. "Is this a conspiracy? First Bridget, then Joyce and now you. Mel, who's to say the man even still wants me? He's footloose. Unfettered. Buying a ranch in Wyoming."

"And you couldn't go with him? You can sell the damn business, you know. And tell me Bridget and Ryan wouldn't be delighted to see you have some kind of life after all these years." Melanie flounced up from the couch and stood in front of the desk, still holding the little package. "Not to mention the fact that if he really wanted you out of his life, Ben Lowell wouldn't be sending you a present." She tossed it in front of Grace. "Go on. Open it."

Grace picked it up and turned it over in her hands. She could feel something square inside. Looking up at Melanie, she said, "Okay. I'll open it but not until I'm by myself. And I promise I'll think about what you said."

"I didn't steer you wrong before, did I?" Melanie grinned. "I practically had to drag you to the rodeo and look how good that turned out."

"All right, all right." She flapped a hand at her friend. "Go on. Give me some privacy. I promise to give you all the gory details later."

Melanie loomed over her. "Will you promise to take off that mental and emotional straitjacket you've worn for the past twenty years?"

"I'll think about it. Go on. I'll call you later."

She practically had to push her friend out the door but when she was gone Grace locked it, sat down again behind her desk and picked up the padded envelope. The return address simply said B. Lowell and an address in Houston. She wondered whose it was. A family member? Another woman? No, he wouldn't do that, send her a gift while spending time with someone else. Would he? And what on earth could be in the package?

Well, Grace, you'll never find out if you don't open it.

Using an antique letter opener she'd picked up at an auction, she slit the top of the envelope and shook its contents onto the desktop. A small square box tumbled out. For a long moment she just stared at it. Finally, her fingers shaking, she undid the wrapping paper and the ribbon tied around it, lifted off the lid and caught her breath.

Nestled in a bed of cotton were a pair of exquisite earrings almost identical to the boot pin. But that wasn't all. Keeping them company was a pair of what could only be called nipple rings, tiny boots hanging from the thin gold circles. She'd never worn them but the stories she read had piqued her curiosity and driven her to do some research on the internet. They were just like the pictures she'd seen.

Her face was so hot she was sure she was blushing, grateful no one could see her.

She turned each item over in her hands several times, feeling the delicacy of the designs. What did he expect her to do with them? Was this some kind of farewell gift? *Think of me when you wear these, so long, it's been good to know you?*

Reaching into the envelope, she discovered a sheet of paper that hadn't fallen out with the box. Fishing it out, she unfolded it and read the note.

Grace,

I looked for a long time to find these, because I wanted to match that pin you're so fond of. Your lucky piece. You are the only woman I've never been able to really walk away from. The one who made me realize how empty my life was before I met you. I'm so sorry you left the way you did, because I think we still have a lot to say to each other. I want to get off the road, Grace, but I want to take you with me. I know you have your life planned out for the next forty years but if the woman who shared my bed with such wonderful abandon is knocking to come out of hiding, I'm here. You know who I am and what I am. Now it's up to you. I'll be in Houston until next Monday. If you show up at the arena wearing the jewelry, then I'll know you're willing to take a chance with me. On us.

Ben

P.S. Age is just a state of mind. I think yours is much younger than mine.

She read the note four times, her body heating, her nipples tingling and her pussy quivering. Spend her life with Ben? Throw caution to the winds? Could she actually do it? Her eyes strayed to the calendar on the corner of her desk. Monday. Three days from now. Turning to her computer, she accessed the site for the Houston Stock Show and Rodeo, checking the standings. Sure enough, Ben was the leading contender in both his events. That meant he'd be competing for the championship again Sunday night.

She nibbled on a fingernail, her mind churning, until she heard the door knob rattle followed by the buzzing of the intercom.

"Grace?" Joyce, of course.

"I'm here."

"Why is your door locked?"

Grace sighed. "Just a minute." She swept the jewelry into the box, stuffed everything into her purse and went to open the door.

"So?" Joyce stood there, a questioning look on her face. "Is everything all right? I didn't know what to think. You never lock your door."

"I'm fine. Come on. Oh, get the calendar first."

Am I really going to do this? Old habits die so hard.

"Okay." Joyce sat down opposite her, the calendar book open on her lap. "What's going on?"

"Check my schedule through next Wednesday. Tell me what I've got that can be postponed until the following week, then see what's left. Look to see who I can hand those things off to."

Joyce studied her for a long moment, obviously changed her mind about asking a question and gave her boss the information.

"That's it," she said when the list was finished. "That should keep things flowing without a hitch."

"Okay. Go ahead and make the calls and have people on standby. I...may be going out of town for a few days."

Joyce stood, her lips fighting a grin. "Please tell me my prayers have been answered. That you're going to do something completely impulsive and out of character."

Grace leaned back in her chair and stared at her secretary. "Am I really such a dull person?"

201

"Oh honey, no." The woman's face was instantly contrite. "You've just held yourself in for so long I wondered when it was going to be time for you."

"Well, we'll see what happens. If I decide to take a short trip, I'll leave a message for you on the machine and your cell. Then you can move forward with this list."

"Do it, Grace." She leaned forward in her chair. "Reach out and grab onto life with both hands. Ride that roller coaster."

Grace gave her a wry smile. "Let's just hope I don't fall off."

* * * * *

She barely slept that night, tossing and turning as every pro and con of the situation battled in her mind. Saturday wasn't much better. First she stood in front of her mirror, naked, juggling the nipple rings in her hand. One site she'd found on the internet had actually been explicit about how to put them on.

Watching herself in the mirror, she pulled and tugged on her nipples, rolled and pinched them until they were swollen and distended. Gingerly she took the first ring and forced the nipple through the tiny circlet. The sight of it was so arousing liquid trickled out to the insides of her thighs and a pulse throbbed in her cunt. When she looked at her face she saw slumberous eyes with heat dancing in them. When she put on the other ring, her body tightened in anticipation of something she knew was currently unavailable.

Damn!

She wished Ben were there to run his hands over her body, to fuck her with his mouth, his hands, his magnificent cock. To order her to her knees and urge her to take his cock into her mouth.

Enough, she told herself, setting everything back on the dresser.

She decided to clean the house to get her mind off her unsettled state. Scouring, polishing and vacuuming every visible surface exhausted her enough so that when night finally rolled around she was worn out enough to fall asleep.

By Sunday morning she was still wavering but she kept hearing everyone's voices in her head. And remembering how she looked wearing the nipple rings. Maybe everyone was right. If she didn't do this, she'd never know what could have happened. She'd turn into an old lady before her time and one of these days even Curt Sanderson would look good to her.

That image was enough to compel her to yank a suitcase out of the closet and pack. She had Ben's cell phone number but this had to be done in person, with no advance warning. Show up, just as he'd said, and hope she wasn't in for an unpleasant surprise.

She left a message for Joyce, another one on Bridget's cell phone. Ditto Ryan and Melanie. Then she pulled up a list on the computer and methodically tried each number. By midafternoon she had the information she needed and was on the road to Houston, decked out in all her boot jewelry.

* * * * *

Ben stopped at Smoky Joe's to have one drink with his friends, Clay glued to his side making sure he didn't repeat the other night. But he had no stomach for another bender or another buckle bunny. Even winning the all-around championship again tonight didn't give him the same high he'd had in San Antonio. He had to give in and admit it. He wanted Grace beyond anything he could ever have imagined.

He'd checked with UPS and knew the package had been delivered but he hadn't heard a word from her. Of course, he hadn't really expected to. If she was coming she wouldn't call first. He hated to think how he'd feel if tomorrow came and he had to pull out of the city alone.

He'd checked the faces in the arena tonight all through the various events, even when waiting to perform himself, hoping he'd catch a glimpse of her. He'd even gone so far as to tell the workers if a woman came looking for him to let him know right away. But he'd finished the night without any sign of her, collected his check, his points and his buckle and trudged off to have a drink he really didn't want.

Clay, who had been his shadow all day, pulled up in front of the hotel to let him out.

"Maybe you should call her," he told Ben, his eyes sympathetic.

"I made my move," Ben told him, "and don't ask me what it was. It's up to her now." He opened the door to get out of the truck.

"Come by the ranch in the morning. You've got three weeks until the next rodeo. You and Hotshot could use a little more R and R."

"I'll see." Ben slammed the door then leaned in through the open window. "Thanks for everything. You're a good friend."

"You're not getting away that easily. I'll call in the morning."

Ben waved at him as the truck pulled away, then walked heavily through the lobby, rode the elevator up to his floor and swiped the keycard in the door, dreading the empty room. The sitting room was dark, although he swore he'd left a light on for when he returned. His mind was definitely not hitting on all cylinders.

He switched on a small lamp and walked into the bedroom, then froze in shock, stunned at what he saw. The bedside lamp was turned low, Lone Star beer was icing in a cooler by the bed and the covers were neatly folded back to the foot. But it was what was in the bed that astonished him the most. In the middle of the bed was Grace, magnificently naked except for jewelry—the pin suspended on a chain from her neck and the earrings and nipple clamps perfectly in place. Her legs were spread wide, her knees bent and she was stroking her cunt with a slow up-and-down motion.

"Holy shit!"

Ben couldn't find any other words. His mouth was so dry he didn't think he could say anything else anyway. His heart was racing and his cock was so instantly hard he was afraid it would poke through the fabric of his jeans.

When he didn't move closer, Grace stopped stroking herself and looked at him uncertainly.

"You said if I wanted to take a chance with you, to show up with my jewelry." She gestured at herself. "Here I am. Or didn't you mean it?"

He finally got his feet unstuck from the floor and moved to stand beside the bed. One hand reached out to touch her, making sure she was real and not a figment of his imagination. Oh she was real all right. He could see her pussy glistening with her juices, feel the softness of her skin, inhale the tantalizing fragrance she wore.

He swallowed. Hard. "Oh I meant it all right. I was just scared to death you wouldn't do it."

"How could I resist an invitation like that?" She watched him carefully. "I wasn't sure if I'd done all this only to have you walk into the room with some other woman. One of your buckle bunnies."

Ben winced. He had no intention of telling her how he'd almost done something he'd regret forever. Nothing happened so there was nothing to tell. And he sure didn't want her to know he was ready to fall into the gutter because he couldn't handle his feelings for her.

His eyes took in every familiar inch of her body. When his gaze landed on the nipple rings, he reached out and touched one of the luscious, ripe buds they encircled, pinching it lightly. It was swollen from being constricted and had turned a dark red that made his mouth water. Impulsively he leaned down and licked each one with the tip of his tongue, drawing a shiver from her.

"Okay." He could barely catch his breath. "Enough chatter. We can talk later. If I don't have you right now I might actually explode."

He toed off his boots, stripped off his clothes and carelessly tossed them to the side, then crawled onto the bed and wrapped Grace in his arms.

"You have no idea how much I've missed you," he murmured before taking her mouth in a ravenous kiss.

He licked the surface of her lips with his tongue, traced their outline then pressed against the seam until she opened for him. When he swept inside he met her small tongue reaching for him, tangling with his. He drank from her, fusing his mouth to hers as if he'd never be able to stop kissing her. Her arms came around his neck, clasping him tightly and her fingers gripped his hair, holding him close.

She moaned in protest when he lifted his head but in the next instant his mouth was trailing down her neck, nibbling behind her ear, placing sucking kisses at the sensitive place where her neck and shoulder were joined, licking across the slope of her breasts. God, she tasted so sweet. When he reached her nipples he bit each one lightly, then soothed them with soft licks. He could have feasted on them all night but he was anxious to taste the rest of her. He couldn't wait to get to her pussy, drink her liquid, fuck her with his tongue.

She writhed and moaned beneath him as his mouth covered every inch of her body, pausing to pay homage to her bellybutton before finally, finally allowing himself to taste her cunt.

Fingers shaking with need, he pulled back the outer lips and avidly licked the pink flesh now exposed. Grace's hips began to jerk and soft little noises rolled from her lips as he bent to his task. He alternated between kissing the sensitive skin and licking it, his thumbs playing a soft tattoo on her swollen clit. His shoulders kept her thighs wide open, giving him easy access to her body and he took full advantage of it.

One finger slid into her tunnel and was instantly coated with her juices. Damn, she was so wet already. He let his tongue take one long, slow swipe at her opening, pinching her clit at the same time.

"Please," she begged. "Oh Ben. Please."

"I'll please you all right," he told her, his voice hoarse. "I'll please you until you don't know your own name anymore."

Reluctantly he dragged himself off the bed, found his suitcase and pulled out the handcuffs he hadn't taken out since he'd left San Antonio. Turning Grace onto her stomach, he cuffed her hands behind her, then pulled her to her knees and propped pillows beneath her to give her stability.

"I've dreamt about this every night," he told her as his hands caressed the smooth skin of her buttocks. "This is mine, Grace. Right? Answer me."

"Yes." Her voice was muffled by the pillows but there was no hesitation in it. "It's yours."

"To do with as I want."

"To do with as you want," she repeated.

"Good." He brought a hand down on one cheek, cock flexing as the skin turned pink. "Tell me you like that."

"Yes. I like that."

He rained light spankings on her until her ass was a pleasant shade of deep pink. Rubbing two fingers through her slit, he smiled to himself to find her even wetter than before. Bending down, he opened her cunt like the petals of a flower and thrust his tongue inside. Grace squealed, jerked, then thrust her hips back at him.

She was going to die of pleasure, she just knew it. Never in her life did she think she would be so turned on by a man's domination. But the very helplessness of her position made her even hotter. Her cunt was so hungry for him she was sure she'd come just from thinking about it, just from the things he was doing to her.

His tongue was like a wicked tool, igniting nerve endings wherever he touched her, and his hands drew responses with their teasing and caressing. And their spankings. God, had she ever thought she'd be ready to beg for spanking, to feel the heat streaking from her ass to her pussy?

Ben was busy kissing and licking the insides of her thighs, his mouth maddeningly avoiding the place she wanted him the most.

"Inside me," she pleaded. "I want to feel you inside me."

He nipped one thigh. "When I decide."

One finger slid into her pussy, then moved back to paint her anus with her liquid. Once, twice, three times, then the same finger pushed against the tight ring of muscle until it was inside her to the knuckle. Grace shivered with need and desire. This man could turn her inside out and she loved every minute of it.

"I'm going to fuck both holes, Grace," he muttered, his voice so thick with desire she almost didn't recognize it.

She heard the snap of latex being tugged into place, then his hands on her buttocks, his knees widening her legs and with one thrust he was inside her pussy. One hand stole around to torment her clit, pulling and tugging on it while he pounded in and out of her.

"Come for me, Grace," he ordered. "I know you're ready. Come now."

And she did, exploding around the thickness of his cock, her body shaking, inner muscles milking him as spasm after spasm rolled through her. She was gasping for breath when she finished but she realized through the fog of her brain that Ben had not climaxed.

Sucking in a breath, she said, "You didn't—"

"No but I'm going to now."

He pulled out of her cunt with wet, sucking sounds, pressed the sheathed head of his cock against her anus, gripped her buttocks and seated himself with one long, hard thrust. She heard herself wail at the intrusion, then her body took over and responded. As he stroked in and out of her she thrust with her hips, trying to time her movements with his.

In and out he moved, delivering the occasional slap to stimulate them both, nipping the heated flesh of her buttocks. When he sped up his movements she knew he was close and she felt her own climax building again.

"Now," he commanded hoarsely and he reached beneath her to pinch her swollen nipples.

The intense pleasure-pain shoved her over the edge and she came again as he pulsed inside her rectum, her body shaking as if it would fly apart. Colors flashed through the blackness surrounding her and every nerve fired and fired again. This was pleasure more intense than any she'd ever felt before. How could she ever have thought she could give it up?

"Mine," he shouted. "Mine, mine, mine."

Ben pumped out the last of his semen and fell forward. She felt the thunderous beat of his heart against her body as her own threatened to pound out of her chest. They struggled to drag air into their lungs, the sounds harsh and raw.

Finally Ben levered himself up, released the handcuffs, turned her over and pulled her against his lean, hard body. His hands slid gently up and down her spine and he tucked her head into the place between his shoulder and his neck.

"Mine," he said again, this time more gently.

She had no idea how long they lay there, content in the silence, bodies sated, at least for the moment. Finally she roused herself.

"I'll bet that beer is good and cold by now."

"I'll get it. But first we need to let those tender nipples free. I think they've been ringed long enough." He worked her

209

nipples free from the rings very gently, then kissed and sucked each one lightly as the blood rushed to the points and pain stung her. But the heat of his mouth soothed everything.

When he was satisfied she was comfortable again, he opened two bottles, handing one to her, then plumped the pillows behind them so they could lean against the headboard.

"I see you liked the jewelry," he grinned. His fingers lifted the boot she was wearing as a pendant. "This started it all, didn't it?"

She wrinkled her forehead. "How did you know?"

"The way you always wore it, kept touching it, as if it were a talisman of some kind."

"A vendor at the rodeo sold it to me. A woman who told me it would help me find my lover."

"And she was right," he said softly, kissing her again. "More than right."

"Wherever did you find the jewelry to match it anyway?" she asked, her breathing finally evening out. "Especially the…the…"

He chuckled. "The nipple rings? That took a lot of searching but I just happened to get lucky." His voice dropped. "In more ways than one."

"Thank you," she whispered, leaning against him.

"Okay. Confession time. How did you find me?"

"That was easy." She smiled at him. "I just called every hotel in Houston until I found where you were registered. Now my turn. Did you win tonight? I was afraid to call the arena and find out."

Instead of answering, he hopped out of bed, fished the buckle and the check out of his jeans and dropped them on her bare thighs.

"Ohmigod!" she squeaked. "You did it. And look at the amount on this check. Ben, you should be able to buy your ranch by now, shouldn't you?"

"That depends."

She frowned. "On what? I thought that was the whole point now. To be able to quit and buy that place in Wyoming. Oh wait. You're going on to Vegas to the Grand Nationals. That should give you what you need, right?"

He lifted one of her hands with his and laced his fingers through hers. "Grace, this has been the most miserable couple of weeks in my life. I never thought you'd get under my skin the way you did. Or…or find a place in my heart."

Her own heart turned over at his words. What was he saying here?

"Are you trying to tell me something?" she asked.

"In my own bumbling way." He took a long swallow of his beer. "I know this has been a big leap for you. I came into your life and turned it upside down. But Grace, there was such a wonderful, sensuous woman just waiting to be turned loose. And now that she is, I don't want anyone else to pleasure her."

She laughed. "I always thought I was being so sensible, so practical, that being in control was where it was at. But my secretary, then Melanie—even my daughter—told me I was about to dry up and blow away. That if I ever wanted to enjoy life I'd better get to you before some other female snatched you away."

And one of these nights I'll tell you about my abortive attempt to settle for Curt Sanderson.

"I'll have to thank them all." He lifted her hands and kissed each finger. "How long can you stay?"

"Until Wednesday." She lowered her eyelids shyly. "If you want me to, that is."

"If I want you to? Are you kidding?" He squeezed her hand. "I want you with me forever. Don't you know that?"

She shrugged. "You never said… I wasn't sure… I mean…"

"Grace." He set both beer bottles aside. "I don't do this very well but I want you in my life permanently. I want to marry you. Can you handle that?"

"And the last of your sexual hang-ups?"

She tilted her lip in a tiny grin. "What hang-ups?"

His laugh was soft and sensual. "But there's logistics to look at. You know, I can buy a ranch anywhere. It doesn't have to be in Wyoming."

Grace shook her head. "No. I want you to buy the piece you've had your heart set on."

"But—"

She touched her fingers to his lips. "Now it's my turn to say, no buts. I need to leave the past behind me, instead of locking myself up in it and away from life. I'm ready to leave San Antonio."

"What about your business?"

She laughed. "As someone pointed out to me recently, selling it will be easy. The house is paid for, so I'll let the kids decide what they want to do with it."

He pulled her across his thighs, one hand capturing a breast and chafing the nipple. "You mean it, Grace? You'd really come with me? It's a big step for you."

Grace took a deep breath and let it out. "You'd just have to be there to catch me every time I faltered."

He lifted her breast to his mouth and sucked briefly on the nipple. "I'll always be there to catch you, Grace. You're mine. That means I'm keeping you forever. If you agree."

"Oh Ben. Of course I do."

"Even knowing the kind of sex life I like?"

She knew she was blushing as she said, "Especially because of that."

He laughed, a full-throated sound. "You little minx. You know, we'll have to send a thank you note to the woman who sold you that pin. Meanwhile, how about sealing the bargain?"

He took one of her hands and wrapped the fingers around his cock, already hard again, as one of his hands began stroking her pussy. "We may never be able to get out of bed," he teased as his fingers drove her toward the peak again.

When he'd rolled on another condom, he knelt between her legs, lifted them over his shoulders and drove deep into her wetness. As he filled her completely, Grace locked her ankles around his neck, touched the pin nestling in the hollow between her breasts feeling its warmth, and wondered why she'd ever been afraid in the first place.

Also by Desiree Holt

~~~
~~~

ℰℴ

eBooks:

Cupid's Shaft

Dancing with Danger

Diamond Lady

Double Entry

Driven by Hunger

Eagle's Run

Ellora's Cavemen: Flavors of Ecstasy I *(anthology)*

Elven Magic *(with Regina Carlsle, Cindy Spencer Pape)*

Emerald Green

Escape the Night

Hot Moon Rising

Hot to Trot

Hot, Wicked and Wild

I Dare You

Journey to the Pearl

Just Say Yes

Kidnapping the Groom

Letting Go

Line of Sight

Night Heat

Once Burned

Once Upon a Wedding

Riding Out the Storm

Rodeo Heat
Scorched
Sedutive Illusion
Switched
Teaching Molly
Touch of Magic
Trouble in Cowboy
Where Danger Hides

Print Books:
Age and Experience (*anthology*)
Candy Caresses (*anthology*)
Demanding Diamonds (*anthology*)
Ellora's Cavemen: Flavors of Ecstasy I (*anthology*)
Erotic Emerald (*anthology*)
Mistleoe Magic (*anthology*)
Naughty Nuptials (*anthology*)
Where Danger Hides

About the Author

ℂ

I always wonder what readers really want to know when I write one of these things. Getting to this point in my career has been an interesting journey. I've managed rock and roll bands and organized concerts. Been the only female on the sports staff of a university newspaper. Immersed myself in Nashville peddling a country singer. Lived in five different states. Married two very interesting but totally different men.

I think I must have lived in Texas in another life, because the minute I set foot on Texas soil I knew I was home. Living in Texas Hill Country gives me inspiration for more stories than I'll probably ever be able to tell, what with all the sexy cowboys who surround me and the gorgeous scenery that provides a great setting.

Each day is a new adventure for me, as my characters come to life on the pages of my current work in progress. I'm absolutely compulsive about it when I'm writing and thank all the gods and goddesses that I have such a terrific husband who encourages my writing and puts up with my obsession. As a multi-published author, I love to hear from my readers. Their input keeps my mind fresh and always hunting for new ideas.

Desiree Holt welcomes comments from readers. You can find her website and email address on her author bio page at www.elloracave.com.

Tell Us What You Think

We appreciate hearing reader opinions about our books. You can email us at Comments@EllorasCave.com.

Why an electronic book?

We live in the Information Age — an exciting time in the history of human civilization, in which technology rules supreme and continues to progress in leaps and bounds every minute of every day. For a multitude of reasons, more and more avid literary fans are opting to purchase e-books instead of paper books. The question from those not yet initiated into the world of electronic reading is simply: *Why?*

1. *Price.* An electronic title at Ellora's Cave Publishing and Cerridwen Press runs anywhere from 40% to 75% less than the cover price of the exact same title in paperback format. Why? Basic mathematics and cost. It is less expensive to publish an e-book (no paper and printing, no warehousing and shipping) than it is to publish a paperback, so the savings are passed along to the consumer.

2. *Space.* Running out of room in your house for your books? That is one worry you will never have with electronic books. For a low one-time cost, you can purchase a handheld device specifically designed for e-reading. Many e-readers have large, convenient screens for viewing. Better yet, hundreds of titles can be stored within your new library — on a single microchip. There are a variety of e-readers from different manufacturers. You can also read e-books on your PC or laptop computer. (Please note that Ellora's Cave does not endorse any specific brands.

You can check our websites at www.ellorascave.com or www.cerridwenpress.com for information we make available to new consumers.)

3. *Mobility.* Because your new e-library consists of only a microchip within a small, easily transportable e-reader, your entire cache of books can be taken with you wherever you go.

4. *Personal Viewing Preferences.* Are the words you are currently reading too small? Too large? Too… ANNOYING? Paperback books cannot be modified according to personal preferences, but e-books can.

5. *Instant Gratification.* Is it the middle of the night and all the bookstores near you are closed? Are you tired of waiting days, sometimes weeks, for bookstores to ship the novels you bought? Ellora's Cave Publishing sells instantaneous downloads twenty-four hours a day, seven days a week, every day of the year. Our webstore is never closed. Our e-book delivery system is 100% automated, meaning your order is filled as soon as you pay for it.

Those are a few of the top reasons why electronic books are replacing paperbacks for many avid readers.

As always, Ellora's Cave and Cerridwen Press welcome your questions and comments. We invite you to email us at Comments@ellorascave.com or write to us directly at Ellora's Cave Publishing Inc., 1056 Home Avenue, Akron, OH 44310-3502.

ELLORA'S CAVE
Romanticon

Annual convention
for women who
refuse to behave

COLUMBUS DAY WEEKEND

www.JasmineJade.com/Romanticon
For additional info contact: conventions@ellorascave.com

Discover for yourself why readers can't get enough of the multiple award-winning publisher Ellora's Cave.

Whether you prefer e-books or paperbacks,

be sure to visit EC on the web at www.ellorascave.com

for an erotic reading experience that will leave you breathless.

Made in the USA
San Bernardino, CA
29 August 2013